BOOKS BY BRENDA S. ANDERSON

THE POTTER'S HOUSE BOOKS

Long Way Home

Place Called Home

Home Another Way

(Coming February 2019)

WHERE THE HEART IS SERIES

Risking Love

Capturing Beauty

Planting Hope

COMING HOME SERIES

Pieces of Granite

Chain of Mercy

Memory Box Secrets

Hungry for Home

Coming Home – A Short Story

Potter's House

THE POTTER'S HOUSE BOOKS, BOOK 11

Place Called Home

A NOVELLA

VIVANT
PRESS

Minneapolis, Minnesota

Vivant Press
Place Called Home
Copyright © 2018
Brenda S. Anderson

ISBN-13: 978-0-9862147-7-6

Scripture quotations are from The ESV® Bible (The Holy Bible, English Standard Version®), copyright © 2001 by Crossway, a publishing ministry of Good News Publishers. Used by permission. All rights reserved.

This novel is a work of fiction. Names, characters, places, and incidents either are the product of the author's imagination or are used fictitiously. Any resemblance to actual events, locales, organizations, or persons living or dead is entirely coincidental and beyond the intent of either the author or the publisher.

Front Cover Design by T.K. Chapin
Back Cover Design by Think Cap Studios

Printed in the United States of America

18 19 20 21 22 23 24   7 6 5 4 3 2 1

Note from the Author

The 21 books that form **The Potter's House Books** series are linked by the theme of Hope, Redemption, and Second Chances. They are all stand-alone books and can be read in any order. Books will become progressively available beginning March 27, 2018.

Book 1: **The Homecoming** by Juliette Duncan

Book 2: **When it Rains** by T.K. Chapin

Book 3: **Heart Unbroken** by Alexa Verde

Book 4: **Long Way Home** by Brenda S. Anderson

Book 5: **Promises Renewed** by Mary Manners

Book 6: **A Vow Redeemed** by Kristen M. Fraser

Book 7: **Restoring Faith** by Marion Ueckermann

Book 8: **Unchained** by Juliette Duncan

Book 9: **Gracefully Broken** by T.K. Chapin

Book 10: **Heart Healed** by Alexa Verde

Book 11: **Place Called Home** by Brenda S. Anderson

Book 12: **Tragedy & Trust** by Mary Manners

Book 13: **Heart Transformed** by Kristen M. Fraser

Book 14: **Recovering Hope** by Marion Ueckermann

Books 15 – 21: To Be Announced . . .

Visit **www.PottersHouseBooks.com** for updates on the latest releases.

To all those who open their hearts
to the hurting and lost
and give them a place to call home.
You make the world a far more beautiful place!

Where we love is home,
Home that our feet may leave, but not our hearts.

~ Oliver Wendell Holmes, Sr ~

Chapter One

After last night, Tessa Chanson wouldn't—she *couldn't*—stay a minute longer. With the noon sun shining behind her, she flung open the front door of the house she'd shared with Jared for four very long years. Her pulse beating faster than a rock 'n roll tune, she slammed shut the door.

Don't turn on lights. Don't leave any noticeable trace that you're leaving.

She cast a quick glance around the black, white, and grey living room. None of the professionally designed decor belonged to her, and she wouldn't want it if it did. Standing in this room was like stepping into a monochrome photo devoid of color. And music. Life.

The only picture of her also had him in it. She'd like to stomp that like he'd stomped her heart.

Stop dawdling, Tessa!

She had a measly ten minutes to pack four years of belongings. Squeezing her hands into balls, she flew past the always-locked den and leapt up the steps two at a time, heading to the second floor. She rushed past one closed door, an empty room Jared once promised would house daughters or sons. Her chin quivered when she passed what should have been the nursery, but she'd shed the last of her tears yesterday.

At the end of the hall, she threw open the double doors to the master bedroom and hurried to the walk-in closet. Oh, she had a ton of clothes to choose from, but the styles and colors had no personality. And all were purchased by Jared. At one time, she'd thought that he was sweet for buying her clothes.

She stepped out of the toe-pinching stiletto-heeled shoes she wore because they matched the image she represented as the hair salon receptionist, and because Jared told her how sexy her legs looked when wearing them. Well, from now on, what Jared thought wouldn't matter. Out of habit, she set them in their cubby in the closet then snagged her brown booties. If only she had a good pair of tennis shoes.

No time to worry about that, Tessa May! No time to change out of her skirt, either. Instead, she hurried to the attic and grabbed her suitcase. She'd carried it into this living arrangement, and she would carry it right back out, and cheer as she did. Her gaze lingered on the dust-covered guitar case that hadn't been opened since the day she moved in. She took a step toward it.

And stopped. She couldn't take it—it would be too cumbersome. Her music had been another casualty of this relationship gone wrong. Starting today, she was finally going to make things right. Once she reached her aunt's off-the-grid cabin, she'd have the independence she craved.

She turned from the guitar and clomped down the steps, returning to the master bedroom. On the hardwood floor, she whipped open the suitcase. If she put it on the bed, she'd leave a telltale sign of her exit.

All she needed to pack were the bare-bones. And the locket. And the picture. She'd never leave those behind. Into the suitcase, she threw one pair of jeans, a couple of shirts, a handful of underwear, and her footie pajamas that Jared hated, not caring if anything wrinkled.

That left plenty of room.

She stole a glance at the bedside clock and grimaced. One minute left? How had time flown so quickly?

She hurried to the master bath scented with a coconut freshener Jared had picked out. Once upon a time, she'd loved coconut. From inside the vanity she grabbed her box of feminine pads. If only Jared knew what she really kept in the box.

She dropped that into the suitcase then yanked open her top dresser drawer. Her heart beat like the drums in a hip-hop tune as she grabbed an item from beneath her underwear.

The ultrasound picture of Cadence. Looking upward, she clamped the picture to her heart and whispered a plea to God to give her baby girl a hug. For Cadence, Tessa needed to escape.

She wrapped a T-shirt around the picture and secured it in her suitcase.

Grab the locket and go!

A clunk sounded below her. Tessa stiffened. Telltale grinding warned her the garage door was raising. He couldn't be home from work. Not yet! It was hours too early.

She jerked open the bottom drawer of the jewelry case on her dresser and stared, slack jawed. Nothing glimmered.

The drawer was empty.

No! Just last week, she'd seen the locket there. Had opened the heirloom, listened to it play "Jesus Saves." Jared couldn't have known she was planning to run. She hadn't known herself until last night.

Last night . . .

She shivered just thinking about it. Had she somehow telegraphed her plans to run? She'd been so careful.

More grinding noise told her the garage door was going down. Jared would step inside the house any second. Her pulse skyrocketed. If she wanted to escape, she had to leave. Now! Necklace or not. Oh, why hadn't she put it on this morning?

Hurry, Tessa! She snapped shut her suitcase and ran down the stairs. She tore out the back door as the mudroom door opened just feet behind her.

If he caught her, she might never gain the courage to run again.

Lungs heaving, she bolted across the small backyard to the alley gate. She squeezed the handle.

It wouldn't budge.

What? She'd tested it yesterday. Had tested it every day for the past year, and never had it been locked.

Wrapping both hands around the latch, she tossed up a long-overdue prayer. "Please, God, help!"

The latch let loose and Tessa tugged open the gate just enough for her to squeeze through. She pulled it shut and leaned against it, her breaths undulating like the bow over violin strings.

"There you are."

Tessa gasped.

Eyes wide, she connected gazes with Caroline, her would-be savior, and nearly cried. Living next door to her had been what had kept Tessa sane for the past year.

"He's home." Tessa's words were a strained whisper.

"Then let's go." Caroline snatched the suitcase out of her hands and jogged toward her garage. Tessa hustled behind her friend, not daring to look back toward the ordinary house that to her had once seemed like a mansion. Growing up on a bus, any home seemed like a palace.

Instead, Jared's house had become an elaborately-disguised prison.

She followed Caroline through her garage door, climbed into the back of the open crossover, and crawled beneath the cover. Caroline slid the suitcase next to Tessa who moved it as far to the right as she could. Then she curled up snug against the seat backs, her head pressed against the luggage, while her friend spread a trunk organizer the width of the vehicle.

"I'm going to put in the stroller too," Caroline whispered.

Tessa heard things being jostled. Something fell and banged against the side of the car. She let out a yelp, then slapped her hand over her mouth.

"Can I help you with that?"

Jared! Had he seen her run? Heard her yelp? If he hadn't heard that, he probably could hear her heart slamming against her chest.

"I've got it, but thanks." A tremble colored Caroline's words.

Tessa tensed. He wouldn't hurt Caroline, would he?

"I insist," he said in that Minnesota-nice way of his that had once made her swoon. Now it made her want to hurl.

"Thank you." This time there was no tremor in Caroline's voice. Whew.

He thrust the stroller into the vehicle, squishing the cargo organizer against her. Tessa cringed, but held in a squeal, remaining silent but for that tattletale beating of her heart.

"By the way . . . " Jared again. The van jostled, but she hadn't heard or felt the hatch close. If she could only see what was going on. *Just shut the hatch, Jared, shut the hatch*, whispered through her brain.

He continued. "Have you heard from Tessa?"

"Tessa?"

Tessa felt something else being thrown in the back. "No. Why?" Silence answered, then Caroline continued, "Could you move please?" Irritation now coated Caroline's words.

"Oh, sorry."

Ha! The only thing he was sorry about was that she'd gotten away from him. So far. Still no sound of the hatch closing. Was he onto her? "But seriously, have you heard from Tessa? She left work early."

How would he know?

Duh! Of course, he checked on her at work. He knew her every move.

"Left work? I don't understand." Caroline sounded genuinely concerned. Who knew she'd be such a good actress? "Look, I don't know what's going on with the two of you, but I have to go pick up my daughter from preschool. I don't have time for your drama."

"Fine." There was the cold tone that sent shivers through her entire body. "I have other means."

The hatch finally slammed shut.

Other means? What did he mean by that? A door opened. The driver's door? Caroline or Jared?

The crossover bounced lightly, and the engine sputtered to

life. But the door didn't close. "If I hear from Tessa, I'll be sure to let you know, okay?" Caroline again. So, it was her in the car, thank God. "I do know she was upset after what happened."

Upset? A tear threatened. She thought she'd shed enough last night to span the entire year.

But Jared? Not a single tear.

"Appreciate it." Something clunked on top of the vehicle. "Drive safely."

"Always." The door closed, and the car lurched backward. Caroline said nothing else—probably wouldn't until they were out of Jared's line of sight—and turned on the radio to a Christian station, one Jared had refused to let her listen to. He didn't want it brainwashing her.

From a man who excelled at brainwashing.

Tessa shivered, though the August temps were nearing ninety. Would he follow them? He wouldn't try to do something to Caroline's car, would he? After last night, she wasn't certain.

The motion of the car shoved Tessa to the left, then to the right, and another right, though not once had she heard the annoying beep of a blinker. Was Caroline trying to shake Jared? Would he have followed them that quickly?

Tessa squeaked out, "Is he following us?"

"Don't know." The car jerked to a stop and Tessa heard what sounded like fingers drumming the steering wheel. "Please tell me you don't have your cell phone on you, do you?"

"Lydia has it." One of the few smart things she'd done before escaping from work this morning.

"Lydia? You gave her your phone?"

"Well, she doesn't know I gave it to her. Yet."

Caroline laughed. "Well played, Tess." The car accelerated, banging the stroller against the back door.

Lydia would know soon, though, once Jared tracked the phone to her laptop bag. Tessa almost felt bad for siccing Jared on her, but the flirtatious stylist had made Tessa's job a nightmare. Maybe she'd see the side of Jared he'd reserved only for Tessa.

Would serve the woman right.

"You holding up back there?"

"So far." Tessa tried to stretch her limbs, but the cargo organizer was jammed too tight against her.

"FYI, I'm driving to Chloe's school first. That way if Jerkwad is following me, he'll see I'm going where I told him."

Made sense. And she certainly wouldn't put it past Jerk— Jared—to trail them.

Thing was, Caroline had told him the truth. She was eventually going to pick up Chloe, albeit, an hour from now. The vehicle slowed and made a turn then came to a stop.

Caroline cut the engine. "I'm running in with Chloe's jacket. Be right back." Another diversion. If Jared was following, would he fall for their ruse? The locks clicked, and Tessa counted out the seconds, while keeping her ears tuned to the world outside the car.

The locks clicked again, and Tessa held her breath as the door opened.

Please let it be Caroline, please let it be Caroline.

"You okay?"

Tessa expunged her breath. "I am now."

Caroline started her vehicle, and once again they were traveling. Tessa hadn't a clue where Caroline was taking her, just that it was out of the metro area. From there, Tessa would have to find her own way to her aunt's cabin. Sharp turns banged her head, then scraped her legs. Every muscle in her body cramped up. Once they arrived wherever Caroline was driving her, unfolding from this balled-up position would take an hour.

"Almost there." The longed-for words were like a sonata to her ears. "And no sign of a red pickup."

She started breathing easier. Had they successfully pulled off her escape?

"We're here." The vehicle slowed and took a sharp turn to the right, then an equally sharp turn to the left. A few seconds later, the crossover came to a stop.

Caroline shut off the radio, and silence filled the vehicle. All except for the thrashing of her heart. What was Caroline waiting for?

"Still no pickup."

Oh, surveillance.

"Let's do this fast." A door opened and shut. A second later the hatch lifted. Caroline pulled out the stroller, pushed aside the trunk organizer, and Tessa slid out. Her legs nearly buckled as she stepped onto the paved parking lot of some no-brand-name motel. She tugged down her skirt then reached into the car to drag out her mostly-empty suitcase.

"You hurry on in." Caroline gestured toward the lobby. "I'll be right behind you."

"Okay . . . " She entered the lobby and looked back at Caroline carrying in a diaper bag. What was that for? She came through the doors and handed the bag over to Tessa. "A few things you might need."

Tessa began to unzip the bag and Caroline laid her hand over the zipper. "Not now. No time. I've got to hurry to get Chloe."

Tessa only nodded and stood back as her friend paid the bill for the night. "I'll repay you."

"Hon, you can pay me by never returning to Jerkwad, got it?"

Tessa nodded.

"And no hitchhiking."

"Yes, ma'am." Tessa hid her hand behind her back and crossed her fingers like she'd done as a child.

Caroline shook her head as if seeing straight through her. Maybe she could. Jared always had. "And when you get to your aunt's cabin, give me a call."

"I promise."

"Good. Now I've gotta go, or Chloe's teacher will ream me for being late. Again."

"Thank you." Tessa squeezed her friend's hand. They said their goodbyes and Caroline hurried out the door. This was going to be goodbye for who knew how long. Jared had once promised to be her savior, instead Caroline had fit that bill.

The problem was, Tessa couldn't remain gone forever, not as long as the heirloom locket was back at Jared's. Once she retrieved that, then she could finally have the independence she craved.

Chapter Two

*T*essa blinked open her eyes then jerked up to a sitting position. Inky darkness surrounded her, stealing away her breath. She hugged herself with bare, goose-bumped arms. Where was she?

Slowly, the room came into focus and realization dawned on her. She'd escaped from Jared and was in a little motel. The clock on the nightstand read 5:00. In the morning? Considering how dark it was outside, it had to be morning, but that also meant she'd slept for over fifteen hours. She'd only laid down to rest her eyes for a minute, not even bothering to get beneath the covers.

Well, that minute multiplied into hundreds more.

Relief bubbled up in her. She'd done it. She'd finally escaped from Jared!

No, twenty-four hours hadn't passed by yet, but this was longer than she'd been free of him since he'd captured her with his broad smile and promises of giving her a home, a real home. Oh, he had, but he'd forgotten to tell her that 'home' had bars. Not the metal kind. No, the emotional kind that were more difficult to break through. Never would she let a man 'rescue' her again.

She stretched and got up from the bed. A shower would

refresh her for the day. Hopefully, this place had shampoo and soap.

Who knew when she'd get to take another shower?

Didn't matter, as long as Jared didn't find her.

Her gaze landed on the diaper bag Caroline had given her. Yesterday, she'd put off finding out what was inside for her minute of sleep, but now curiosity overwhelmed her. She carried the bag from the dresser to the bed and unzipped it. Her hand flew to her chest. Caroline had thought of everything.

One of those prepaid cell phones, with Caroline's number programmed into it. Energy snacks. Scissors? A refillable water bottle. A rain poncho and a small flashlight. Oh, and hair color similar to her natural red. Now the scissors made sense. Would Jared recognize her without the long and straight chestnut-colored hair he'd 'loved' on her?

One more thing hid in the bottom of the diaper bag. A book. Tessa pulled it out.

A Bible.

Oh, Caroline. Tessa didn't deserve a friend like her.

Faith had been another thing that Jared had stripped from her. Truthfully, she'd gladly handed it over during those first few months with him when he'd rescued her from her crazy life on a bus. What she'd give to go back to that kind of crazy.

Only lately had she begun to hear God's whispers again.

She opened the Bible to the middle where Psalms was usually found.

And something fell out.

A ten-dollar bill?

She paged through more of the book, and more money

floated from the pages. She sniffled but refused to let tears fall. She was going to be stronger now. On her own, she'd have to be.

She hid the bills back inside the Bible then retrieved her box of feminine pads from her suitcase. Saying a prayer, she removed the pads from the bag. She unfolded one from the bottom, and her shoulders unknotted just a hair. She checked six more and relief filled her. The money—usually fives and tens—she'd been hiding in the folds of her pads, for the past several months, hadn't been discovered. The pads were one thing Jared never touched.

Thank God she'd had the foresight to hide money there. She'd done one thing right anyway.

Now to take care of her hair that reached halfway down her back.

She went into the bathroom and stared at the familiar image, the one Jared had created. Long, brown, straight hair that looked nothing like the curly red God had gifted her with. Well, it was time to return to who she was.

She cut off a good five inches so that her hair fell just below her shoulders, then spent the next hour on the dying process.

When complete, Tessa checked the mirror again. The woman who looked back at her looked like an old friend, one she hadn't been in contact with for far too long. How had she let Jared convince her that coloring her hair and straightening it would make her look more beautiful?

It hadn't.

And even when she'd transformed herself into the image he wanted, he still hadn't been satisfied.

But that was all in the past. He would not hold control over her anymore.

The sooner she got to her aunt's cabin, the faster she could get on with life.

Once she left here, reaching her destination would probably take days. The air would be cooler in the morning, so if she started early, she'd hopefully be able to travel further in one day. Too bad she didn't have extra money to splurge on a pair of walking shoes. Her feet were not going to be happy. But if getting away from him meant enduring a little pain, it was worth it.

She packed her meager belongings and dressed in her same clothes from yesterday. The jeans she'd brought along would be too hot for the walk today.

But before she began her journey, she needed to find something to eat. Would this little motel have anything? She hadn't paid attention when Caroline checked her in.

She walked toward the lobby, her heart pulsing as she peeked around very corner before making the turn. Just off the lobby, she found some plain donuts and orange juice, just enough fuel to carry her through a few hours. Then, with her suitcase in one hand and the diaper bag in the other, she set out on the road to independence.

Nate Brooks closed his Mac and tucked it into his backpack. He had better hit the road now or he'd get stuck in the massive trails of cars heading north for the weekend. Who knew he'd be this excited to go to his parents' place? And no picking up strays along the way, either. Why God had given him the desire to help homeless young adults, Nate would never know. It had been a blessing he hadn't seen coming.

He stretched out the kinks in his back. Sitting in this unforgiving booth wasn't the most ergonomic way to work, but the office rent was the right price. Free. And all because he'd taken time to listen to the owner of Brandt's Burgers, Brats, & Beer.

Huh. So, his parents had been right about the importance of listening. Actually, he was learning that they were right about a whole bunch of other stuff too. How was it he'd felt so smart and grown up during high school and college, and now that he'd graduated, he was discovering how little he knew. Guess that was all part of growing up.

Just like paying the bills was a part of being an adult. Especially those student loan bills. Ugh! Which was why the word *free* was one of his favorites.

He flung the backpack over his shoulder, and walked past booths filled with downtown Minneapolis business men and women. Definitely a different clientele than he saw in the evening when he did his Uber driving. Around noon, people were generally still sober. The darkness and anonymity of nighttime seemed to bring out the worst in people.

But it also gave him the opportunity to be God's hands and feet.

Another 'huh' moment. He never would have predicted he'd be sharing the gospel with others, especially to the bar crowd. But really, weren't the people who came here at night seeking the same thing as those who attended church on Sundays?

He headed to the bar and waved down Werner Brandt.

Werner set a cola in front of Nate and, as always, refused payment. But Nate always tried.

"You're heading out early." Werner said in his thick German accent as he wiped condensation from the varnished bar top.

"Yep. Dad and I are working on my bus. It's plumbed, now we need to build some walls and cabinets."

"It's going to be a regular home."

Nate grinned. "That's the goal." Renovating that old school bus had been one of his proudest achievements in his young life. It had survived its first road trip a few months ago, including the run-in with the deer and the breakdown in the middle of Chicago. He was itching to take it out again, but with his new job, vacation time was a long way off.

He took a gulp of his Coke. "If I can build up enough graphic design business on the side, I could work anywhere. Just take The Draken and travel."

"And if you meet a nice young fräulein along the way?" Werner moved over a bit as a server set a plate filled with a burger and fries in front of Nate. All free. Another reason for him to keep coming here.

"Nah." Nate waved his hand. "My uncle was over forty when he got married, and he landed a winner. I plan to be just like him." He'd been girl-crazy in high school and even somewhat in college, but after what happened to Bridget . . .

Nope. Not going there.

Nate bit into the sandwich and moaned. He could grill a pretty mean burger, but something about eating food someone else cooked always made it taste better.

"You like?"

"Amazing as always." Nate licked grease from the side of his mouth as he debated bringing up a tough topic. He decided to go ahead. If Werner didn't want to talk about it, he wouldn't. "So, tell me, how'd your meeting go yesterday?"

Werner's eyes lit with a sparkle Nate seldom saw. The man had gone through a lot, much of it his own doing, but he'd survived. He pulled over a stool and sat across the bar from Nate. "I saw my daughters yesterday."

"You did? And how did they react?"

The light faded from Werner's eyes. "They were scared." And rightfully so. Werner had not been a kind father. Supervised visitation was the best he would likely ever have of his daughters, but that was more than he said he deserved. "But they will see me again. And they're why I need to sell this place."

"What? Why?" Werner loved working here. He'd even become a minister of sorts to those nighttime drinkers looking for a listening ear, seeking hope in their broken lives.

"Gina." His ex. "She says as long as I work at a bar, she won't trust me." Werner's shoulders stooped. "And I can't say I blame her. Alcohol turned me into a demon. How can I serve to others who might be hurt the same way?"

"Couldn't you just skip selling beer? I mean, no one makes a burger or brat like you do." Nate took a huge bite of his burger and moaned his pleasure, to prove his point.

"*Nein*. The food might be good but the patrons, they expect their booze to wipe away their troubles. I can no longer serve them a lie."

Nate heaved out a breath. Wanting Werner to keep this place was purely selfish. "Then all I can say is, I'm happy for you."

"And no worries, young man." Werner nodded to the booth reserved especially for Nate on Fridays. Monday through Thursday, he worked long days to get in his forty hours, so he could have Friday to work on self-contracted graphic design. "That booth is yours, no matter who buys this place. It's in the contract."

"You're too good to me, Werner."

"No, young Nate. You saved me."

The praise never sat well. All he'd done was listen to a broken man and then tell his own story. Just like he did for many Uber passengers, and many young people he picked up *just because*. God had done the rest. "Uh-uh, God saved you."

But why hadn't He saved Bridget?

"Yes, yes He did."

Nate shook off thoughts of Bridget and finished off his burger. "You'll be here next Friday, though, right?"

"That is the plan."

"Then I'll see you in a week. Gotta go give my Draken some love." And if he left now, he wouldn't have to worry about running into more destitute-looking people that God nudged him to pick up. First, he didn't have time to pick up anyone, and second, just last night he'd been warned by Our Home's administrator that there were no rooms available. Nancy would have his head if he brought home anyone else. Death by Nancy would not be pleasant.

Still, he grinned at the thought. Really, she was a softie who knew the exact amount of mothering to give anyone who lived at Our Home, the home for homeless young adults.

He kept his head down as he left the bar. Stopping to chat with someone would eat up too much of his time. He walked around to the backside of the building where Werner always saved a free parking spot for him. He got into his ancient pickup and started it up. Without making any stops along the way, he should make it to his folks' place in less than two hours, then he and his dad could spend the weekend working on The Draken. His dad seemed to have just as much fun working on the old school bus as Nate did.

Traffic was heavy in downtown Minneapolis, thanks to road construction that never seemed to end, but he still made it onto the highway heading west in ten minutes. He stayed on the freeway for many miles, then veered off onto another that was already backed up with travelers heading north.

No problem, he knew the side roads. He exited the highway as soon as he could. It added miles to his trek, but at least he wasn't going five miles an hour, sitting in fender-to-fender traffic.

To make time go faster, he turned on the truck's radio and sang along with it. No one was around to complain about his bad singing voice. Just because he couldn't sing didn't mean he didn't appreciate good music when he heard it.

The truck climbed a hill and movement way up ahead caught his eye.

A hitchhiker.

Don't look. Don't stop. Just drive right on past, Nathan.

Rather than slow as he approached, he pressed the accelerator harder. It was a woman. In a skirt and heels. From the back, she looked young.

Nope. Don't think of it, dude. There are no rooms available at Our Home, remember?

He sped past her and looked in the rearview mirror.

Oh, man, she was young. Probably about his age. And pretty too, with reddish wavy hair flowing past her shoulders. That was reason enough for him to keep going. He kept his gaze focused ahead, but he couldn't shake the image of her.

Walking in heels. That had to be tough on the feet. What if her car had broken down? He could just give her a ride, couldn't he? Wouldn't that be the gentlemanly thing to do, as his parents had taught him?

He growled as he slammed his foot on the brake. Just once, couldn't he head up to his parents' place without a distraction? Why couldn't he just once ignore God's nudges?

Because guilt would eat him up if he did.

He put the truck in reverse and looked in the mirror.

She was gone.

Huh?

Trees lined both sides of the road. Had she stepped off after he passed her? Was her disappearance a sign that he should keep moving forward? If he kept going, he'd be home in just over an hour.

But . . .

God's familiar nudge told him to back up, so that was what he did until he reached the spot where he'd last seen her.

The young woman had vanished.

But she'd left behind a diaper bag.

Chapter Three

Tessa thrashed through the woods, her heart feeling as if it would pound right out of her chest. How had Jared found her?

She leaped over a fallen tree, but her heel caught on a branch, wrenching her ankle, and sending her flying face first to the earth's floor.

She got to her knees and tried to stand, but shocking pain plunged her back to the ground.

No. No. No! She did not get this far only to be dragged back to Jared's prison. Not without a fight anyway. She got up on her hands and knees and crawled forward, trying to ignore the searing pain in her ankle.

"Hello," a voice called out.

A male voice that wasn't Jared's. She stopped and listened.

"You forgot your diaper bag," the stranger's voice said.

No. It was a trick. Jared probably brought a friend to coerce her back. Well, she wasn't falling for it.

She kept crawling forward, trying to avoid thin branches that would break and alert her captor. Her knees now screamed for relief, right along with her ankle.

But she would not cry. She would not give up.

"Hey, are you okay?" The voice was much closer this time.

Too close.

She searched the ground for a steady branch to use as a cane.

"Can I help you?"

Hide. Her knees and ankle screamed out as she crawled toward a nearby bush.

And then his arms were around her.

Screaming, she flailed against him, beating him, scratching at his face.

And he dropped her. "Hey, hey, I'm just trying to help."

She rolled over and looked up into blue eyes while scooting backwards, trying to keep her sore foot suspended. "Leave me alone. Tell Jared I'm not coming back."

"Whoa." He held up both hands. "I don't know any Jared. I just thought . . . " His gaze flitted to her knees, then her ankle. "You're hurt." He knelt beside her. "Listen, I don't know anything about this Jared guy, but I do know your ankle needs help. It's the size of a cantaloupe. You won't get anywhere until it's taken care of."

She tried pushing off one more time and the pain in her ankle brought tears to her eyes. This stranger was right, she wouldn't get anywhere.

Jared had won.

She sniffled and wiped her nose. Life with him wasn't that bad, really. They lived in a house that could fit twenty people, let alone two. He never hit her. She always had food. Clothes. Medical care.

She just didn't have love.

Or freedom.

Or Cady.

"Fine." She swallowed a knot in her throat. "I'll let you help, but you can tell Jared that the first chance I get, I'm out of there."

The skinny, blond-haired young man shook his head and rolled his eyes. "Whatever you say." He took off his polo and a T-shirt, then slipped the polo back on. He ripped the T-shirt a few times, giving him several long ribbons of material. "I'll secure your ankle."

He dug through the fallen leaves on the forest floor, then picked up a semi-flat stick. He wrapped that with one of the shirt shreds.

"This might hurt." He secured his hands below her knee and behind her calf and lifted.

She squeezed her eyes shut as he balanced her leg on his knee. Her skin tingled with pain where his hands touched.

"By the way, I'm Nate." He untied her shoe then removed it. "I don't know anything about medical care, but I'm assuming we should immobilize this."

Pain knifed up her leg as he secured the swathed stick to her leg with T-shirt fabric. She clamped her teeth together to keep from yelling out.

"Sorry." He winced but kept wrapping. "I'll get you to the doctor."

"No!" she shrieked. "Absolutely no doctor." They'd ask for insurance, and then Jared would find out where she'd been, and he'd somehow track her.

"But—"

"No." She crossed her arms.

"Whatever." He finished wrapping her ankle, then stood. He looked back at the trail they'd created, then down at her.

He scratched the side of his face. "Um, I'm gonna have to carry you."

"No!" She wrapped her arms around herself. "I can—" She attempted to stand, but even with the ankle wrapped, pain still screeched, and she collapsed on the ground. "Okay," she grunted out, making sure her skirt was tucked tight between her legs.

He knelt and put one arm below her knees and braced the other behind her back. "Hang on."

Every inch of her that he touched tingled and pleaded to be let loose, so she squeezed her arms tighter around her own shoulders.

"Listen." He remained kneeling. "If you don't want me to drop you, I need you to hang on."

"But—"

"I'm serious."

"Fine." Cringing, she wrapped her arms around his neck and every nerve ending zinged. She closed her eyes and tried to imagine herself embraced by a rocking chair.

Without even a grunt, he stood, raising her off the ground. Huh. The skinny guy must be hiding his muscles.

"Don't worry. I toss eighty-pound hay bales in the summer, and you're almost as light as they are."

Right. She snorted. That was why Jared had always ragged on her to lose weight.

"Oh, and there's your luggage." He nodded to the suitcase wedged in a bush, and the diaper bag up ahead. "I'll get them after you're settled in my truck." He carried her out of the woods toward his red pickup.

The one she'd assumed was Jared's.

Seeing it up close, it wasn't anything like Jared's. This one was old and had dents and rust spots. Jared had taken better care of his truck than he had of her.

"You really don't know Jared?"

"Nope. But I do know that I'd probably like to punch his lights out."

Caroline's husband had said the same thing. Repeatedly.

And Tessa had defended the jerk.

No more.

Nate lifted her onto the passenger seat. "Wish we could elevate your leg somehow."

Her too. Ankle throbbing with pain, she buckled while he retrieved her luggage and the diaper bag. He tossed them beneath the bed cover then got in and started up his truck. It shook like an unbalanced washing machine and growled like an injured lion. This pickup sure didn't purr like Jared's either.

How could she have been so stupid? She hugged herself, shivering. One glimpse of a red pickup had sent her running and then royally messed up her ankle. She looked down at it, but her skinned knees drew away her attention.

"You cold?" He fiddled with some buttons and the cab instantly heated up. "Can I at least know your name?"

She looked down at her lap and muttered. "Tessa."

"Jessica?" He pulled out onto the road.

She cleared her throat. "Tessa."

"Oh, sorry. Tessa. Nice to meet you. I'm glad God put you in my path."

Did he really believe that? Caroline would. "Me too," she finally said.

"So, no doctor?"

"Please."

"If that's what you want." He shrugged. "Where were you headed? Can I drop you off there?"

She looked out the window at the trees whizzing past. Even if he would bring her all the way to Auntie Shay's, she wouldn't be able to survive on her own with this injury. Unless by some miracle, her world-traveling aunt was at the remote cabin. And if she was, would she even let Tessa stay?

"I was going to Bemidji, but . . . " She looked down at her wrapped ankle. Why had she been so reckless? If she hadn't run, her ankle would be fine, and riding with Nate, she'd have taken miles off her walk.

She heard him haul in a breath then heave it out. "If it's okay with you, I could bring you to Our Home. They can take care of you there."

Say what? "*Your* home? *Who* will take care of me?"

"Oh, sorry. Our Home is a place for homeless young adults. Now I don't know if you have a home or not, but hopefully they can put you up for the night anyway. The counselor's a former police officer. She'll know basic first aid to take care of your ankle and knees. Get you up and moving about on your own really quick."

"Is it a shelter?"

He shrugged. "Not really. It's an actual house people live in while learning to be on their own. My aunt and uncle used to live there until God pointed them in a different direction. Now everyone who lives there calls it home. And Nancy, the administrator, is also everyone's mom, and believe me, she treats you like one of her kids." He grinned. "Not always a good thing."

"Sounds wonderful." She mumbled to herself, playing with the hem of her skirt. Wasn't a real home what she'd always wanted? What she'd thought Jared would be giving her? Maybe there she could learn how to be free. "You can take me."

"At your service." He drove up to the next intersection and pulled a U-turn. "That means backtracking a bit, but we'll be there within an hour. If you want, take a nap."

As much as she would have like to sleep, the suspicious part of her warned her to stay awake.

"Mind if I turn on music?" He reached for the radio knob.

"It's your truck."

"Yeah, but I don't want to upset you any more than you already are. If you'd like music, I'll turn it on. If you'd prefer quiet . . . "

"Music's fine." Tessa stared at the young man as he turned on his radio, to a Christian music station at that.

Would she hear anyone that she knew? Her parents maybe? Would she recognize their voices anymore?

His fingers tapped the steering wheel to the beat of the music, and he started humming along—if that was what you could call it.

"Oops, sorry." He shrugged. "I like music, but everyone says my singing could make a laughing hyena cry."

A chuckle escaped her throat, and she covered her mouth. How could she think of being happy when her world had turned inside out?

No surprise, thoughts of what she'd fled from wiped away her glimpse of joy, and for the remainder of the ride, she stared out the window, watching trees and fields zoom past.

Within an hour, they turned off the main road onto a blacktop driveway that split years-old pine trees. The trees peeled away, and a two-story house came into view. Not quite a mansion, but it was still huge. Jared's home had nothing on this place. A front porch spanned the entire front of the house, beckoning her to sit on the swing and read a book.

Wouldn't it be nice to read a book of her own choosing once again?

Maybe God really had heard her recent prayers. Maybe she was about to find a real home.

Nate parked the truck in front of a three-stall garage, then he came around to her door and lifted her out.

Every cell screamed with his touch as he carried her onto the porch. He nodded toward the swing. "Mind if I put you there for now? I first need to talk with Nancy, the administrator."

"I'd like that." She'd be able to sit and smell fresh air and listen to nature and not worry about being late with supper.

Nate set her down, and she stretched out her leg on the swing. Under his breath he said, "It's not going to be pretty."

What did that mean? Warning signals went off in her brain, and every cell in her body screamed. What if he was one of those human traffickers? With her injured ankle, she had no way to escape.

Voices drifted through an open window behind her. Nate and some woman. Examining the landscape around her, looking for a means of escape, Tessa attuned her ears to the conversation.

"But she's hurt." This from Nate.

"Nathan Brooks, I warned you this morning we didn't have any beds. What am I going to do with you?"

Did that mean Nate was telling the truth about this place?

"Then where do I bring her?"

"You have the list of recommended shelters."

So, this place was legitimate. Did that mean Nate could be trusted?

"But—"

"But nothing. I have to follow rules here, or we'll be shut down. I'm sorry."

"Yeah, I know, but can Kathy take a look at her ankle? She's got some pretty scraped-up knees, too."

A sigh floated through the window. "I'll call her down."

Didn't matter if this place was the real deal or not. It was full, and now she'd have to go to some shelter where Jared would certainly find her. She hugged herself and glared at the sky. It figured, things weren't going to go her way. Clearly, God was still punishing her for running away with Jared. Away from parents whose only sin had been sheltering her too much.

Nate grunted as he stood, but Nancy didn't flinch as she ended her call to the counselor who lived upstairs. Nothing he had to say would change her mind. She was too much like his own mom. Still, he'd give it one more try. He intentionally sighed and looked Nancy in the eye. "I was certain God told me to pick her up. I mean, I even drove past her because I heard you in my head, but . . . but I couldn't keep going. He wouldn't let me."

She just smirked. "Too bad God didn't inform me I should break the rules."

Nate groaned.

"Oh, Nathan, you have a good heart, but you're a bad actor."

"I had to try." He shrugged.

"Tell you what . . . " She got up from her office chair, came around the desk, and wrapped him in a hug. Then she stepped back and held him at arm's length. "Just because I said 'no' doesn't mean God did. I trust your nudges, Nathan. They may irritate me at times, but they've never proven wrong. Just remember, this is one closed door. Look for the open one."

"Okay," he said while sighing. Naturally, she was right.

"Now, let's go meet this young woman." She took his arm, and they walked outside. The counselor was already out there, talking with Tessa, and by the scrunched look on Tessa's face, the news wasn't good.

Nate stood a few feet away, his hands tucked into his back pockets. "What's the verdict?"

"Well, I'm not a doctor." Kathy smiled at Tessa then looked up at Nate. "But judging by the swelling and bruising and her inability to put any pressure on it, my guess is it's more than a sprain. She needs to see a doctor ASAP."

"But—"

Kathy laid a hand on Tessa's arm, silencing her. "It's not an option, not if you ever want to walk right again."

Tessa looked upward, blinking, and she rubbed a finger over her nose. "Fine. But somewhere in the cities."

Nate stepped toward her. "No problem."

"And . . . " Kathy stood, set a hand on Nate's arm, and

looked him in the eye. "Give your Aunt Debbie a call."

"Gotcha." Aunt Debbie was a licensed therapist who'd just returned to work after years of being a full-time mom. She'd know how to talk to Tessa. After she gave him a hard time for picking up another stray.

But he couldn't help it.

He checked his watch. By now, he should have been at his folks' place. There went the evening of working on his bus. His dad would be disappointed.

Nate was disappointed. Since graduating, he'd actually come to enjoy the time with his dad. The man was wiser than Nate had ever given him credit for.

But they'd have all day tomorrow and most of Sunday to work, that is, if he got Tessa to the doctor right away, and if they could fix whatever was wrong tonight. Which meant he had to leave now.

The question then was, where did they go after seeing the doctor?

He knew of one place but didn't like it.

And he wouldn't be the only one.

Chapter Four

With Nate by her side, Tessa crutched her way out of the Twin Cities' area clinic, her foot temporarily splinted while the swelling went down.

Seven entire weeks before her fractured ankle would be healed enough to walk without a splint, cast, or boot. Eleven or twelve weeks until she'd be back to normal, and then only if she was faithful with therapy. In one week, she had to have surgery. That meant wherever Nate dropped her off, she'd be stuck for weeks.

By the time she had her freedom, Jared would have received statements from the insurance company. She shivered. Would that lead him to her?

She tried shaking the thought as Nate helped her into his pickup. He'd been silent much of the time since they'd left Our Home, as if in deep thought, or maybe prayer. What she did know was that he didn't seem too thrilled to be stuck with her, that picking her up had messed with his plans.

If only she hadn't panicked when she'd seen the red pickup slow down.

He drove out of the parking lot and turned onto a busy

road.

"I'm sorry I've caused so much trouble." She looked straight ahead at a road leading to where, she didn't know. Once again, she was at the mercy of a man. "What happens now?"

He drummed his fingers on his steering wheel, and his jaw worked back and forth as if he was unsure of his plan. "I've got a bus."

A bus? Her head jerked his way and a glimmer of joy lit inside her. "You mean an RV type of bus?"

"Yep." He shrugged. "It's a work in progress. Has electric and plumbing, but not a lot of walls yet."

"And you'd let me stay there?"

His fingers continued drumming. "Unless God suddenly gives me another idea, yeah."

"Cool."

"Cool?" He turned his head her way then immediately back toward the road.

She splayed her hands over her skirt, straightening it. "That's how I grew up."

"On a skoolie?"

"That's what they call them now?"

He shrugged. He seemed to do that a lot.

"So, yeah, a skoolie." She looked out the window as fields of corn streaked past. How many different vistas had she seen growing up when she'd longed for a stable home. "My family . . . we were . . . they are . . . were . . . musicians."

"Were?"

"I don't know. I haven't spoken with them." Not since she'd run off with Jared, the man who'd promised her that stable home.

"You haven't looked them up on the internet?"

"No." That was another freedom Jared had taken from her. Actually, she'd given it up freely because he'd warned her how dangerous it was. Her parents had said the same thing, so she hadn't questioned him. How stupid she had been. She looked down at wringing hands. "Does your bus have Wi-Fi?" Maybe she could finally learn to use it. Banning it had been one thing Jared and her parents agreed upon.

"Not yet, but you can use . . . " He scratched the side of his face and heaved a sigh. "You can use it in my parents' house."

"The bus is on their land?"

"Yep. In a shed. Dad and I were going to work on her this weekend."

Ahh, so those were the plans she was screwing up. "I'm sorry."

"Hey, no reason to be sorry. You didn't ask for this. We're just gonna make the best out of the situation." He flipped on his blinker and turned onto a long asphalt driveway surrounded by maple trees beginning to don their fall colors.

"This is beautiful."

He blinked then smiled. "Yeah, I guess it is." He shrugged. "It's home."

"Wait." Dread electrified every nerve ending in her body. "Do you live in your bus? If so, this won't work." She'd rather pitch a tent in the middle of nowhere than share a home with some man again.

He laughed as he parked his pickup in front of a three-car garage. "Oh, I agree, it wouldn't work. I live and work in the cities. I was just coming home for the weekend to work on The

Draken."

"The Draken?"

"Yep. As in dragon. It's named for a Viking long ship that traveled from Europe to the US. I plan to take it around the states." He opened his door, and she followed suit. "Just stay there. I'll give you a hand."

He hurried around the pickup. He removed her crutches from the tiny seat in back and handed them to her before helping her out of the truck. Like a perfect gentleman, just as Jared had been. He still behaved that way, when it served his purpose. At least she'd learned to be watchful and wary.

Nate led her toward a large, inviting deck and gestured toward one of the patio chairs. "If you wouldn't mind sitting here. I need to talk with my parents, and it's not going to be fun."

What did he mean by that? Every indication he'd given her said he led the idyllic home life.

As had Jared.

When would she stop reading signals wrong?

All she knew was that she wouldn't stay here one second longer than she had to. As soon as she could put weight on this ankle, she was out of here.

Nate inhaled a breath before entering his parents' house. They were not going to be happy. Yeah, he'd told them he was arriving late, but Tessa would be a surprise. No doubt, they'd jump to conclusions about their relationship, just as they'd done in the past.

In the past, though, he'd given them good reason to reach those conclusions. He was no longer that hormonal young man. Bridget had cured him of that for good.

As usual, he found his mom in the kitchen, baking.

"Hey there, whatcha making?" He aimed his finger toward her mixing bowl, and she swatted his hand with her wooden spoon.

"Nathan Brooks, you know better than that," she scolded, but there was a smile in her voice. "Come down here, and let me kiss you."

He bent over, and she reached up on her tippy toes to give him a kiss on his cheek. She might be short, but he didn't dare cross her.

"Now you can sample." She dug a table spoon into the batter and handed it to him. "It's a new peanut butter dip I'm trying."

He tasted the dip, and his eyes rolled back with pure pleasure. "It's a winner." Just like everything else she made. Her baking business had taken off a few years back, so now the house was always filled with mouth-watering aromas. If he hung around home, he might actually gain some weight. His dad sure had.

On cue, Dad entered the kitchen, the newspaper clutched in one hand, and his reading glasses in the other. And he didn't look happy. Uh-oh.

Dad set the newspaper and eyeglasses on the island, then craned his neck toward the window that overlooked the deck. "Something tells me we're not going to get a lot of work done this weekend."

"What?" His mom twirled toward him then turned toward the window. "Nathan Brooks," was all she said as she shook her head.

"It's not like that. We're not dating." He gestured to the stools by the island where a plate of fresh cookies waited to be sampled. "Can we talk?"

His parents shared one of those clairvoyant looks that seemed to communicate pages of thoughts, then his mom said, "We're listening."

"Okay, here's the deal." He handed his dad a cookie before telling them about today's adventure. When finished, he took a cookie as well. "So now, she needs a place to stay until her ankle gets better."

"And you figured The Draken is that place?" His dad crossed his arms and gave that stern look that made Nate want to sink into the floor.

But he wasn't backing down. "Yep. Our Home is full. She can't get the proper medical care at a shelter. Where she was heading, she'd be by herself."

"You're going back to the cities on Monday, right?" Mom sat on the stool beside him.

Well, there was that issue. He took a bite of his cookie and gave an exaggerated groan of pleasure. "Mom, these are the best oatmeal-raisin cookies you've ever made."

She only shook her head and removed the cookie plate from the island then stood by his dad. "Your flattery will get you nowhere, young man." But she smiled. "Is there something you need to ask me?"

He gulped and stuck his hands in his back pocket. "Would you mind . . . would it be okay if Tessa stayed in The Draken during the week? Would you mind looking after her? Please?" He ended with a big, fake smile.

"There's one thing you haven't explained." His dad got up, poured himself a coffee, then returned to the island and sipped at his drink without clearing up his statement.

And Nate's smile dissipated. What had he missed? Was his dad going to say 'no' to Tessa staying there? If he did, where would she go? Aunt Debbie's house maybe? With three kids, they had no extra room. "What?" Nate finally squeaked out. "What did I miss?"

His dad held his coffee between both hands. "She's running from something or someone. Why? She's obviously frightened. Is she in danger?"

Nate shook his head. "I don't know." He hadn't considered the answers to any of those questions. He'd just followed his gut reaction to pick her up.

"Okay, then maybe this is something the police should handle." His dad took a sip of coffee.

"But Kathy talked with her at Our Home when she was checking out Tessa's ankle. She didn't say anything."

"Kathy's no longer a police officer," his mom said.

"But wouldn't she have said something if it was serious?"

"I can't answer that." His dad retrieved the plate of treats and stuffed a cookie into his mouth. "I'm worried that if she's running from someone, that *someone* might be a danger to our family."

"Oh." Nate slumped. "I hadn't thought about that."

"That's because you have a big heart." His mom came around the island and hugged him. "You always want to see the best in people."

"I'm sorry." The last thing he wanted was for some madman to show up at their house. He and Dad could handle it. Maybe Josh. But Mom and Jaclyn? "What do we do?"

His parents shared one of those telepathic looks again, then, as usual, his mom delivered their message. "She can stay for the weekend. That'll give you time to do some research, see where she can go. Don't forget to ask Aunt Debbie for advice."

"Thank you. I'll let Tessa know." He stood.

His mom laid a hand on his shoulder then wagged her finger. "How is it you get yourself, and us, into these situations?"

"I don't know." He grimaced and raised a shoulder. "Just lucky, I guess." He sure hadn't been looking for trouble, but it always seemed to find him. He turned toward the door. "Let me introduce you."

"One minute." His dad's stern tone stopped Nate.

Now what? Nate looked back at his dad.

He stood next to the island, arms crossed. "Just to confirm. There's nothing going on between you two."

"What? I just met her earlier today, and honestly, she's got issues I don't want to touch, so no, there's nothing going on now, nor will there be in the future." Been there. Done that. Never again. "I'm just, you know, trying to listen to what God tells me to do."

His dad gave one slow nod, but still hadn't smiled. "Just make sure you're listening to God and not your hormones."

"Seriously?" Nate shook his head and stalked out. You'd think his dad would trust him by now. Nate had absolutely no intention of falling for Tessa. He didn't need that kind of complication in his life.

Chapter Five

essa petted a black kitty that had wandered onto the deck then found a resting spot on her lap. She'd never had pets, growing up on the road or at Jared's home. Maybe once she got to the cabin, she'd have a kitty just like this one. Maybe the cabin would be as restful as this place appeared to be.

She turned to the house behind her. What was going on inside? Nate had been in there a while, and to be honest, she was perfectly fine with that. For the first time in years, she felt a sense of freedom and out here, at this country home, Jared was a million miles away.

A door slammed behind her, and Nate stomped out.

Did that mean she had to leave?

Following close behind were a man as tall as Nate and a woman who had to be a foot shorter than the two.

Nate stopped by her chair and petted the cat who purred beneath his touch. "I see Falcon found you."

"Falcon? Um, I think you have your animals mixed up."

He grinned. And it was a pretty nice grin at that. "Named for Falcon, a superhero in the Marvel comics and movies. I was never big into comics, but I like the movies."

"Oh."

"You don't watch them?"

Staring off at the treelined driveway, she ran her hand over the cat's silky coat. "No." Nate didn't need to know that Jared wouldn't let her watch movies, unless he was watching John Wayne. He'd warned her how bad movies were for her, and she'd never had the gumption to stand up to him.

She looked Nate in the eye. "I'd like to see them though."

He grinned. "I can make that happen."

Someone cleared their throat, and Nate stepped back while combing fingers through his curly blond hair. At one time, she would have thought him cute. Jared had cured her of finding any man attractive.

"Mom, Dad, this is Tessa. Tessa, these are my parents, Janet and Marcus Brooks."

"Nice to meet you, Tessa." Janet pulled up a chair close to her and the men sat in other chairs on the deck. "Nate tells us you've had quite the day."

That was one way to put it. "I guess so."

"You're welcome to stay the weekend."

Tessa let out a breath she hadn't realized she was holding. "Thank you. I don't know where else I'd go."

"That's something you can research this weekend. We've got Wi-Fi in and around the house."

A lot of good Wi-Fi would do with no computer. Tessa pictured the Star Trek-like flip phone Caroline had given her. She wouldn't be doing any research on there either. "Um, I don't have a computer or a smart phone."

"Silly me." Janet slapped her forehead. "I'm sure Nate has an old laptop he can let you use." Her gaze flicked to Nate.

"Yeah. No problem."

Hope fluttered inside Tessa's belly. Maybe she could finally research her parents' music group. Would they let her come back?

Janet briefly touched Tessa's hand. Boy, this family was touchy-feely. "And you do not have to stay out in that bus. You're very welcome inside the house. Our oldest daughter has moved away from home, so her room's available."

"Actually." Tessa ran her teeth over her lower lip. "I wouldn't mind staying in The Draken." She'd looked forward to it even, hoping to resurrect good memories.

"If that's what you'd prefer, though it probably won't be easy to maneuver with your ankle."

"I can do it."

"Then I'll make sure Nathan brings you fresh linens—" Janet fired a gaze at Nate "—after he cleans up the bus."

Tessa focused on her splinted ankle. Jared would mock her for being such a burden. "I don't want to put you all out."

"We wouldn't offer if we didn't want to do it." Nate's dad finally spoke. There was a gruffness in his voice, but she didn't feel reprimanded. Instead, she felt embraced, a feeling she hadn't had since she'd left her parents.

Why had she taken their love for granted? Why hadn't she been satisfied with the life they'd given her? Sure, they'd been old fashioned, but at least they'd loved her.

So, why hadn't they ever contacted her?

She banished those thoughts. If she truly wanted to be independent, then she had to stop feeling sorry for herself and make the best out of what she was given at this moment. Her parents had imparted that wisdom to her, it was time she took it to heart. Mustering a smile, she looked from Marcus to Janet. "Thank you. I'm indebted to you." And to Caroline and Nate.

"You can pay us back by enjoying a warm meal." Janet gestured toward the grill. "How would you like a burger?"

Her stomach rumbled at the very idea. She hadn't eaten since that small breakfast at the motel this morning. "I would love a burger." How was it she felt loved by these people she'd known for only a few minutes? The same way Caroline loved her. And the same way her parents had loved her.

Maybe Auntie Shay's cabin wasn't her final destination.

Maybe she'd already reached it.

Seriously, Tessa? A few minutes with this family and she was already putting them on a pedestal? That was the exact same thing she'd done when she'd run away with Jared. She hadn't realized then how blessed she was to have parents who loved her.

But if they loved her, why hadn't they answered her letters?

Out of the corners of her eyes, she watched Nate whispering to his father. Whispers meant secrets which were never good.

This time, she wasn't going to be fooled by a friendly smiles and too-good-to-be-true offers. As soon as she could get away and be on her own, she was out of here.

Chapter Six

Pain throbbed through her ankle as Tessa limped alongside Nate toward the big pole shed illuminated by the setting sun. She needed to take some meds, get off the leg for the night, and elevate it. And then sleep. Tomorrow she would wake refreshed and ready to show this family she was more than a sympathy case.

It would help if she really believed that. But the sooner she healed, the quicker she could move on and find a home and prove to the world she could be strong.

She stole a glance at the young man walking beside her. He'd treated her like she was important. So had his parents. Although the meal tonight had just been burgers and grilled potatoes, she hadn't tasted something so delicious in forever.

Also, over dinner, she'd learned he had a sister who lived in New York and a younger brother and sister who were gone to some camp for the next week. Were they anything like Nate?

He walked alongside her, carrying her suitcase and the diaper bag. The only time Jared had helped her was those first few months of living with him, and then only when trying to impress others.

Was that Nate's plan too?

She wanted to believe this family was the real deal, but she couldn't afford to let down her guard.

Nate opened the door to the shed, and she blinked to adjust her eyes to the dim light.

"There's The Draken." Pride rang in his voice as he gestured to his bus in the middle of the shed that also housed a boat, a tractor, a bunch of wood, and other machinery. The bus was painted a deep purple with a huge dragon's head on the side.

Wow! "Did you paint it?"

"Yep. Turned out good, if I do say so myself."

"Is that what you do for a job? Paint?"

"Well . . . sort of." They walked slowly across the cement floor toward the bus. "I'm employed as a graphic designer, so in a way I paint, but it's with a computer instead of a paintbrush."

"You're talented."

He shrugged. "Just doing what God created me to do."

God again. "You do that a lot." She stopped moving.

"Do what?" Looking back at her, he cocked his head.

"Talk about God." Was that what made him seem different? She leaned heavily on her crutches, trying to ignore the pain in her ankle. "How *He* told you to pick me up. How *He* created you. My parents were believers. I was a believer—"

"Was?"

"These past few years . . . " She looked toward the ceiling, then back at Nate. "But I never believed like you do. Maybe that's why it slipped away so easily."

He snorted. "Mine hasn't always been this strong either.

Just ask my parents. It took a tragedy to get my head on straight." He rapped the side of his head with his knuckles then hurried to the bus and opened the door before she had a chance to ask more questions. So, she wasn't the only one running.

She hobbled the final feet to the bus and was exhausted by the time she got there. Who knew walking with crutches would be so tiring? She stared at the steep steps leading up. How would she climb them? The narrow stairway wasn't big enough for Nate to lift her again, for which she was grateful.

"Just a second." Nate disappeared onto the bus. A light came on inside, then he returned with a stool. "This should help. I'll stand behind you to make sure you don't fall."

Jared never would have thought of a stool, or if he had, he wouldn't have bothered.

She handed a crutch to Nate, then using the other for leverage and grabbing the railing alongside the steps, she pulled herself up. True to his word, Nate stayed behind her, with a hand bracing her back. She took the next step, and another, without problem.

One more to go. One hand holding the crutch, the other gripping the rail, she leaped up.

And fell backward. *Ahhh.*

Her scream was stopped by Nate's strong arms wrapping around her waist.

"Gotcha." How could she feel so secure, yet ache with his touch? He gave her a gentle push to the bus platform. "Told you I'd catch you." There was a grin in his voice. Jared would have chastised her for being clumsy.

Oh, yeah, she could fall for Nate Brooks, but no way was

she going to let that happen.

He gestured to a captain's chair to her left. "Have a seat. You can see anything important from here." He pointed to a dinette table and bench seats across from her. "I'll turn that down to make a bed. I've got a bunk in back, but I'm guessing you don't want to climb up there right now."

"Oh, aren't you the smart one?" She teased back then stiffened. Just like Jared had always told her, she never learned.

Thankfully, Nate didn't respond to her tease. Instead, he quickly converted the dinette area to a bed by removing the tabletop and the metal legs. Then he placed the tabletop where the legs had been and put an extra cushion on top, squeezing it in between the bench cushions, and voilà! he had created a bed. He topped that with sheets, blankets, and pillows he'd brought out earlier.

He walked to a cabinet midway to the back, right in front of a plywood wall with a doorway cut through it. "I've got some munchies in the cabinet." He bent down to a dorm-sized fridge and pulled out a bottled water. He tapped the plywood wall. "Behind this is a compost toilet plus a shower and sink. No doors yet, just curtains. Our plan was to build walls this weekend."

And she'd ruined those plans. She hugged herself. "Don't let me stop you from working. I'll stay out of your way."

"You sure?" He rejoined her at the front of the bus and handed her the water. How'd he know she was thirsty?

She stared out a bus window at the dusk-darkened shed. "I've ruined your day enough as it is."

"Ruined?" He sat on her bed and brushed a hand through

his hair. "You didn't ruin it, you just added color. I'm learning that when God sends me on a detour, I need to enjoy the view." For some reason, that statement didn't bring out his smile.

And made her want to know more. "How many detours has God sent you on?"

His lips tilted up to the right. "Enough to let me know that He's in charge, no matter how long that detour is." He slapped his hands on his thighs and stood. "Well, I suppose I should let you get some sleep. If you need anything, just call my cell." He pulled out his phone. "What's your number? I'll call it, then you'll have mine."

"It's 763 . . . " Uh, no, that was her number on the phone she'd left behind. A flip phone that had allowed her to do nothing but make phone calls. Nate didn't need to know about that. "I don't know." She pointed to the diaper bag on the dinette. "I've got a new phone, new number."

He handed her the bag and she dug through it and found the phone at the bottom. Yes, it was still a basic flip phone, but this one Jared couldn't track and couldn't control who she called or who she received calls from. She flipped it open and stared at the small screen. How did she find the number? When it came to technology, she was a complete idiot.

"I can help." He held out his hand, and she sheepishly handed him the phone. Now he'd know she was stupid and helpless.

Seconds later, a song played from Nate's phone. "Got it." He handed the phone back to her. "Now I'll call you, and you'll have my number."

An electronic tone played from her phone.

Which reminded her to call Caroline, let her know she was safe, and find out if Jared had bothered them again.

Her hands shook at the thought of him, and she dropped the phone. He couldn't find her here, could he?

She clenched her fists, banning the worry. He might control her back at his house, but he would not control her here.

She bent down to pick up her phone and bumped heads with Nate.

"Oh, sorry!" Flinching, she sat upright. "I didn't mean to . . ."

But he laughed. "Hey, don't worry about it." He handed her the phone. "If you need anything, I mean *anything*, call me."

"Thank you," she said softly. Those two words hardly expressed her appreciation.

"Glad to help." He walked to the steps and touched a toggle switch on the bus wall by the door. "Here's the light switch." Then he gestured toward the door. "There's a deadbolt on here, if that would make you feel safer."

"It will. Thank you."

He left the bus and an eerie silence took his place, making her shiver in spite of the humid warmth permeating the air. She leaned over a bar by the door and, stretching out as far as she could without putting pressure on her already aching ankle, she managed to turn the deadbolt.

Now to take some pain meds and then call Caroline. She found Ibuprofen in the diaper bag and downed two with the water. Then she shut off the light before climbing in bed and elevating her foot. After getting comfortable, she took out the phone, found Caroline's number in the contacts, right beneath

Nate's, and hit 'call.'

It rang only twice before she heard her dear friend's voice. "Are you okay?"

Tessa laughed. Caroline always got right to the point. She filled in her friend on running from Nate and the fractured ankle and surgery. "Now I'm in a safe place. Nate's family has taken me in for the weekend—"

"Whoa. You're staying with strangers?"

"Yeah, well, they're super nice and they're Christians." She knew that would make a difference to Caroline.

"Uh-huh. And probably axe murderers in disguise."

"No. Really. They're good people." Even though she had her suspicions, she wanted to reassure Caroline, so she wouldn't worry. "And the guy who rescued me, he's really cute and talented and kind—"

"So, just like Jared was when he *rescued* you from your life on the road." Caroline sighed. "Come on, Tessa. Use your head! You thinking Jared was your savior was the very thing that got you stuck with him. Now you're doing the same thing with this family."

"But these guys are different. You can even look them up online." She sat up and, from the diaper bag, she dug out a business card Janet had given her. "They're MarJan Homes out of Brainerd."

"Oh, you better believe I'm going to research them."

"I knew you'd have my back." She took a sip of water, dreading the answer to her next question. "Any word from Jared?"

Breathy silence replied. "He stopped by our house three times today, nearly in tears, swearing he doesn't know what he'll do without you and that he'll change. Blah, blah, blah."

Tessa closed her eyes but couldn't drum up sympathy for him. Not anymore. She believed he really was remorseful, but never enough to get help. Besides, he'd played those I-can't-live-without-you and the I'll-change cards so often that she knew those promises would last about a week before he reverted to his controlling ways.

"And what did you tell him?"

"I played dumb. He doesn't believe me, of course, but it doesn't matter. He won't get a word out of me or my hunky-hubby."

Tessa laughed, and they said their goodbyes. Oh, to have a genuinely caring relationship like Caroline and Mitchell had.

Someday maybe. But first she had to learn to live on her own.

The pain jutting through her ankle told her that would be a while.

She laid down, set the phone within reaching distance, and closed her eyes. Tonight, she would have sweet dreams.

Suddenly Jared's tear-filled face was plastered to the windshield. He was kneeling and his fingernails, sharp as a tiger's, were scraping at the window, carving a hole in the glass. The windshield broke and fell onto the driver's seat.

Tessa awoke with a scream.

Chapter Seven

*N*ate lay in his old bed in the room he once shared with his younger brother, Josh. He missed that kid. Hard to believe they once fought like a dog and a stray cat.

His folks would have said Nate was the cat as he'd always been the instigator of problems. Just like today.

Although Tessa was a different kind of problem.

What was God doing now? And why did He keep choosing Nate? Couldn't one weekend go by without some kind of drama? And more setbacks to his traveling-the-states dream?

He punched his pillow. As much as he wanted to, he couldn't stop hearing God's voice. Couldn't *not* listen. He'd learned the hard way what happened when he closed his ears.

He lay on his side and looked out the window facing the backyard. A yard light glowed above the pole shed, but the lights inside the shed were dark. Was she sleeping well?

What was her story? What or whom was she running from?

And why did she have to be so cute?

Bridget had been cute too, but that cuteness had masked more problems than he could deal with.

He closed his eyes, shutting out the yard light. If he wanted to get any productive work done this weekend, he needed to get some sleep.

His cell phone trilled out a generic tone and Nate jerked up. Better not be a telemarketer at this time of night. Not opening his eyes, he felt for his phone on the nightstand and knocked it on the floor between the bed and stand.

Klutz!

He tried squeezing his arm between the two pieces of furniture, but they were too close. This room had always been too small for two guys.

The tune sang on as he got out of bed and followed the phone's light. It had wedged between the headboard leg and the floor molding and the night stand. He couldn't have put it in a more difficult-to-reach spot. If this was a telemarketer, the caller was going to get an earful.

Finally, he snagged the phone, and it went silent. Of course.

He looked at the caller I.D.

Tessa!

Drat. He hit 'call' as he pulled on shorts.

"Nate?" She sounded breathless. Terrified.

"You okay?" Not bothering to put on a shirt, he ran from his room, phone at his ear.

"I . . . I don't know. Something's scratching the bus—I think someone's trying to break in."

"Be right there. Stay on the line."

His parents' bedroom door opened ahead of him, and his dad peeked out. "What's going on?"

"It's Tessa." He tore past his dad. "Someone's trying to break into The Draken."

"Right behind you."

With his dad practically on his heels, Nate flew down the steps, taking two at a time. He fumbled with the deadbolt, then flung open the back door and leaped over the deck steps to the ground. His heart beating faster than a galloping horse, he flew across the yard toward the pole shed.

His foot sank too low on the next step, some animal-dug hole, and Nate's leg crumpled, sending him face first to the grass, and the phone flying off to who-knew where. He'd find it later. He scampered up and raced toward the shed. He reached for the handle.

"Wait there, Nate." His dad called from too far behind. "We don't know what we're facing."

"But—"

"Nathan Brooks." The tone stopped him like some magical spell. He looked back at his dad running with his Remington 30-06, one hand on the rifle's forearm, and the other hand on the trigger guard.

Nate gulped and waited at the door. His dad gestured for him to flatten himself against the side of the building while he did the same.

Gun in one hand, Dad grasped the doorknob, turned it, then slammed open the door.

Birds flew and squawked.

Then silence.

Dad raised a finger to his mouth then reached inside the building, turning on the lights. They flickered then lit up the entire room.

Nate saw no movement and heard nothing but the pulsing of his heart and his dad's heavy breathing. Slowly, they crossed the floor to the bus, their heads on a swivel, watching for any movement.

Something rustled on the other side of the bus. "There!" Nate pointed toward the driver's side tire.

"Get behind me." His dad growled. He raised his rifle and peered through the scope, his finger at the ready. "Whoever's there, come on out. The police are on the way."

They were?

Nate felt for his cell phone and realized it was somewhere on the lawn. What he'd give to have their German shepherd back to take down who- or whatever was in here. Rex had died only a few months ago, and no one had the heart to replace him. Maybe it was time to rethink that.

Rustling again.

His dad tracked the movement with his rifle and fired.

A curdling scream pierced the air. Nate ran to the bus and tugged on the door.

Locked.

He pounded on it. "Tessa. You're safe." His heart slowly decelerated as he waited for her to unlock the door. Once she did, he skipped the steps and leaped right to the platform.

Tessa sat on the bed, hugging herself, shivering.

"It's okay." He dug a blanket out of the cabinet beneath the dinette bench and draped it over her shoulders. Behind him, he heard his dad climb the steps. "It was a raccoon. Nasty thing."

She stilled. "A raccoon? But I thought I saw . . . " She shook her head. "No. It was a dream. And then I . . . I panicked." Her gaze slid to her hands fidgeting in her lap. "I'm sorry. Again," she muttered.

"Nothing to be sorry for." Dad laid his rifle on a shelf above the windows then sat in the captain's chair. He drew a hand down his whiskered face. "But I do think it would be better for you to stay in the house. Lauren's room's on the second floor, but there's a bathroom next to her room."

"Lauren?" She looked from Dad to Nate.

"My sister in New York."

"Oh."

Nate gathered her suitcase and diaper bag. "I can carry you up the stairs."

She shivered. "Uh, I can do it myself."

What was her problem with being carried? "There are a lot of steps."

"And I have a whole bunch of determination." Tessa grabbed her crutches.

"Guess I can't argue with that." Nate gestured toward the door.

"One more thing." His dad nailed her with a gaze that hopefully conveyed she wouldn't want to cross him. Nate had tested it so often, he still had the mental bruises. "Tomorrow, young lady, if you want to stay here this weekend, you will tell us what you're running from."

Nate could see her shaking. What kind of monster had she fled?

And what kind of danger had he put his family in by bringing her here?

Chapter Eight

Tessa awoke to the morning sun peeking through a crack in the blinds, and panic gripped her. What would Jared say about her sleeping in?

She threw off her covers and a weight on her foot stopped her from hurrying from bed.

Then reality hit.

She wasn't at Jared's anymore.

She was safe.

Or was Caroline right, that she was trading one bad situation for another? Somehow, this place felt different, but she'd be stupid to not be on her guard.

Just like she'd be stupid to throw away this opportunity to spend a few days in an actual home, not some shelter. She lowered both legs over the side of the bed and reached for her crutches, wincing as blood rushed to her formerly elevated foot.

She could do this. Her gaze settled on her suitcase and she groaned. Jeans would be too difficult to put on, but she'd worn that skirt two days in a row. Well, Jared wasn't here to criticize her wardrobe, so today would make three days.

Would this family be willing to drive her to town, so she could pick up more clothes? Maybe there was a second-hand store that wouldn't eat up much of her piddly savings. She was already asking so much of this family, but the worst they could say was 'no,' and she was used to hearing that. That is, *if* they allowed her to stay once they heard her story.

With a little effort, she managed to slip on her skirt and shirt, then headed to the bathroom right next door. Time spent there wasn't any easier than getting dressed. And now she had to maneuver the long set of stairs.

Using her crutches, she made her way to the top of the steps and looked down. The stairs seemed to sway and whirl, and her stomach threatened to heave. Visions of Jared pushing her, then grabbing her just before she fell, flashed through her memory.

A hand gripped her shoulder, and she screamed.

"Whoa." Nate pulled her back from the steps. "You okay?"

She fell back against Nate and shook her head against his solid chest before jerking away from him. "Everything was . . . moving."

"Then let me help you down." Not letting go of her shoulder, he stepped beside her, linked his arm with hers, and took one of the crutches. Needles seemed to puncture her arm where he held on, but that was better than falling. Firmly in his grasp, she gripped the railing and hopped down one step. Twelve more to go, and she was already exhausted. Nate was going to be so angry about how long she was taking.

Her teeth clenched so tight her jaw ached, she hopped down another step. Eleven remaining. At this rate, it would take her fifteen minutes to go down one flight of stairs.

"You're doing great, Tessa. Take your time."

Say what? She angled her head toward Nate, making sure he was serious and not mocking her.

He grinned and gave her a thumbs-up. "Our goal is to get you—and me—down in one piece, so take all the time you need."

She smiled back. And somehow that took away her fear of taking the next step, and the next, until she stood safely on the hardwood floor. If she could have, she would have done a victory dance. Instead she offered Nate a sincere, "Thank you."

"My pleasure." He handed her the second crutch then gestured to the kitchen table where his mom and a strange woman sat chatting. "I've been volun-*told* to make breakfast this morning. What would you like?"

"You're asking me?"

He shrugged. "Why wouldn't I? You're a guest."

She stared at Nate as he headed into the kitchen and plucked a red pan from a pot rack hanging over a large kitchen island. Not once while growing up, and definitely not while living with Jared, had she ever been asked what she wanted for a meal.

"Scrambled eggs are fine." That should be easy and wouldn't cause him too much trouble.

"Scrambled eggs coming up. Mom? Aunt Debbie?"

"You're cooking." Janet raised her hands in the air. "So make whatever you want. I'm going to enjoy being pampered."

"Me too." The other woman, Nate's Aunt Debbie, linked her hands behind her head and sighed.

"Come sit down, hon." Janet pulled out a couple of chairs and motioned toward them. "Your job this morning is to stay off your feet." She patted the chair beside her. "This afternoon, we're taking you shopping."

Her gaze jerked to Janet. With all this jerking, she swore she'd suffer from whiplash. Were these people real? Or was it all a ploy to draw her in, like Jared had, before revealing their true selves?

She sat across from Nate's aunt who extended her hand.

"I'm Debbie, Marcus' sister."

"She's a counselor." Nate set a pitcher of juice and three glasses on the table.

"Yes, I am, but today I'm here as a friend. We just want to ensure that not only are you safe, but that this family is safe."

"Me too." The last thing she wanted to do was bring danger to others, not that Jared was dangerous, but . . .

"Do you mind if I ask a few questions?" Debbie wrapped a hand around her juice glass.

"No." But that didn't mean Tessa planned to answer all the questions or give them more information than was absolutely necessary.

"I understand you've had a traumatic couple of days."

Tessa nodded as Nate set plates and silverware in front of them.

"Do you feel safe?" Debbie laid her hands on the table, palms up.

Tessa looked over at Nate, then at Janet and nodded again. Speaking would give too much away.

"That's good." Debbie took a sip of her juice. "Did you feel safe before coming here?"

Tessa covered her mouth with her hand and gulped. "Jared never hit me."

Debbie nodded this time. "That's good. Jared—he's your husband?"

"No. He was my boyfriend."

"And you lived with him?"

Tessa looked down at her lap and mumbled, "For four years." Oops. Why did she offer that?

"Can I ask why you're running from him?"

How to answer . . . She didn't want to get Jared in trouble. With her out of his life, maybe he'd revert to the Jared she knew at the beginning. She looked out the dinette window at the expansive backyard that would be perfect for a child to run and play in. "I was heading to my aunt's cabin."

"Is she expecting you?"

"No. The cabin's off the grid." Which was why the cabin was the perfect spot to hide. And Auntie Shay was rarely there, from what her parents had told her.

Of course, she hadn't heard from any of them since she'd run off with Jared, so everything could have changed.

"I see." Debbie smiled. "How about writing her a letter?"

"I don't have her address." Which was true, but Tessa was certain she could find the place again. Besides, when it came to letter-writing, she'd written probably a hundred letters over the years, but not a single one had been answered. Her family had never forgiven her for running away. This from a traveling gospel group who shared the news of Jesus' forgiveness to anyone who listened.

Hypocrites.

But Auntie Shay had been different. She believed in

nothing but herself.

"But you do have her name and the city her cabin was in."

Not a question, but a statement, as if Debbie could read Tessa's mind. It made no sense denying what she knew, so she nodded once again.

"Well, enough of that." Debbie took a napkin from the holder at the end of the table.

And Nate scooped spoonfuls of eggs onto each plate. Then he set a bowl of cut-up fruit in the middle of the table.

It may have been just eggs, but they smelled delicious. Tessa picked up her spoon to dive in.

"Nate, would you say grace?" Janet asked.

Tessa put down her spoon and folded her hands. Once upon a time, praying before meals had been as natural as breathing. Jared had taken that from her as well.

"Dear God, thanks for this breakfast and for time with Aunt Debbie this morning and for bringing Tessa to us. Keep her safe and let her know she's loved. In Jesus' name, Amen."

Debbie and Janet echoed with their own Amens. Tessa waited until the others picked up silverware before attempting to dig in again.

She took one bite, and her eyes rolled back. Yes, it was just eggs, but she hadn't had to make them, nor were they cooked by some fancy chef as an apology from Jared. Besides the burgers last night, she hadn't tasted anything this delicious in years.

"Excellent job, Nate." Debbie scooped fruit onto her plate. "What are your plans for the day?"

Nate spooned a second helping of eggs onto his plate. "Dad and I are gonna put up some walls in The Draken, then maybe set up the projector for movies tonight." He looked at Tessa. "What do you like to watch?"

She shrugged. "I don't know." As a teen, she'd rarely gone to movies, and then they were only blatantly-Christian movies. And Jared, he never asked what she wanted. Instead he made her join him to watch John Wayne re-runs. "Anything but John Wayne or westerns."

"Not a problem." Nate grinned. "You said you'd watch Marvel movies, so I've got just the one for you."

She resisted rolling her eyes. Nate was just like Jared, choosing movies for her. But this time, she knew better than to fall for a handsome face and slick speech.

Small talk ensued from there. Debbie praising Nate's brother for working with her daughter in some theater production for special needs kids. Nate bragging about the website design he was doing for some lawyer friend just opening his office. Janet showing off pictures of her kids and all her nieces and nephews.

They were all treating Tessa like she was a part of the family. The thought of going to some women's shelter on Monday made the eggs curdle in her stomach. If only she could stay here until she could head north. How could she prove herself invaluable when she had no skills beyond housekeeping and cooking or answering a phone at a hair salon? And with her bum foot, cooking and cleaning were out of the question now too.

"Are you all right, Tessa?"

She shook her head and looked across the table at Debbie whose eyes seemed to penetrate her mind. Well, if that were the case, she might as well lay her thoughts and feelings on the table and see what happened.

She folded her hands in her lap and made eye contact with everyone around the table. "I want to know what I have to do to stay here until I can go to Auntie Shay's. How can I help?"

"That's not a question I can answer without talking with my husband," Janet reached an arm around Tessa.

She recoiled and tried to hold in the grimace.

Janet drew her arm away. "I assure you I'll put in a good word."

"Me too," Nate said, his mouth full of fruit.

"As will I." Debbie gave her a thumbs-up. "But know that my brother can be a tough nut."

"Until then, let's get you shopping." Janet collected the plates and brought them to the sink. "I'm volunteering Nate to clean up."

Nate groaned. "Volun-telling you mean."

"So, what did you guys decide?" Nate was barely in his dad's office before spewing out the words to his dad, mom, and Aunt Debbie. That was all he'd thought about while working with his dad, while showering, while setting up the movie for the evening. And now that Tessa was taking a bath upstairs, he could finally ask.

"Have a seat." His dad motioned with his head toward an open chair, then raised his hand toward Aunt Debbie. "You want to fill him in?"

Nate swiveled toward his aunt. "Well?"

She smiled, which was reassuring. If she were about to deliver bad news, her face would warn him. "As you know, she's a wounded young woman."

"Yeah, but she said he didn't hurt her."

"No, she said specifically that he didn't *hit* her. And that use of word was intentional."

"Oh." He slumped.

"She doesn't like to be touched," his mom added. "I tried putting my arm around her, and she practically jumped out of her skin."

He'd noticed that too. And with his touchy-feely family, that had to be hard for her.

"She also doesn't have a lot of confidence." Aunt Debbie folded her hands in her lap, a signal to him that they'd reached a verdict.

"But she's brave and independent." Nate leaned toward his aunt. "That has to mean something."

"Absolutely it does. I'd love for her to talk with one of my colleagues."

"So, does that mean she can stay?"

"Why is this so important to you, Nate?" Dad leaned forward.

"It's not. Actually, it puts a crimp in my plans. I didn't get half done today what I wanted to."

"Yet, you're still going to bat for her. Why?" His dad swung an imaginary bat at an imaginary ball.

Good question. Nate scratched the side of his head. "Because . . . " Because of Bridget, that was why, but he couldn't voice his feelings out loud. He knew exactly the reaction that would get. "Because she has nowhere else to go, and I can't keep her in the condo, that's against Uncle Ricky's rules." Having a woman stay overnight would be an instant eviction from his sweet housesitting deal.

His dad frowned, clearly not buying Nate's excuse.

"There's more, Nate."

He squinted at his aunt.

This time, she didn't smile. "Tessa has lived in an emotionally abusive situation, and I get the impression that things were escalating. She opened up a bit more while shopping. No, he didn't hit her, but he almost knocked her down the stairs at least once. He's raised his fist to her, threatening but not following through. He's broken things of hers, including something that was very valuable, but what she didn't say, but I do know it hurt her deeply. And there was more. The fact that she ran says a lot about where she anticipated his behavior was heading."

Debbie took a sip of water and cleared her throat. "But that's also why letting her stay here can be a risk. Domestic disputes are some of the most volatile and dangerous situations for a couple and for anyone who tries to step in, including the police."

"Can she call the police now?"

"That's one option, and we've provided other resources for her, but not much else can be done without her consent. Right now, she doesn't want him hurt."

He raked both hands through his hair. "I don't get it. Why do people protect abusers?"

Aunt Debbie sighed. "There's a too-long psychological explanation for that, but for Tessa it boils down to him not physically harming her."

"But he could."

"Yes."

Nate turned to his dad. "Does that mean you're kicking her out?"

Dad shared one of those looks with Mom again.

This time, Mom spoke. "We're going to allow her to stay as long as she wants. But if there's a hint of danger, all that will change. I will not put our family at risk."

"Yeah, I get it. And I promise to be out here every weekend until she can move out." He planned to be here anyway, working on The Draken. As long as she didn't get in the way, that would work.

"Mmm-hmmm." Mom laid a hand on his arm. "One more thing."

He cocked his head toward her. "Yeah?"

"This young lady might be broken, but she's also very pretty. Please guard your heart."

He snorted. "Believe me, I've had my fill of messed-up women. It won't happen again." And even a well-adjusted woman would wreck his plans to travel around the country. He looked at his parents and Aunt Debbie. "So, we're good?"

"Unless something changes. Yes." Dad splayed his arms, giving Nate permission to leave.

He hurried upstairs to retrieve his phone from his bedroom. Electronic gadgets were never allowed in family meetings, and he swore his folks had some kind of sensor in the office that tattled when a phone was brought in. Over the years, he'd learned the smartest thing to do was leave his phone in his room.

Phone now in hand, he thumbed a text to a friend while

walking past the bathroom. He jerked to a stop. Music? Not radio or iPod. No, this was the most angelic voice he'd ever heard, singing some song he didn't know. The music magnetized his feet to the floor. He leaned against the wall, closed his eyes, and listened.

Okay, maybe he hadn't been truthful to his parents. He'd only known Tessa one day, but to say he wasn't attracted would be an outright lie. And now that he'd heard this voice like a siren, he knew now more than ever that it was good he'd be returning to the cities tomorrow. His stupid heart could easily fall for her.

Chapter Nine

Why did bathrooms always have the best acoustics? With Tessa's broken ankle resting on the side of the tub, she couldn't resist singing one of the songs she'd sung with her parents, a love song to Jesus. But she'd changed it up. She'd gotten rid of the bluegrass sound and turned it into a ballad. They hadn't let her perform her version.

And Jared had banned her music completely.

So, to sing here, freely? She even meant the words.

A knock on the door shut off her song. Praying it wasn't Nate knocking, she cleared her throat and said, "Yes?"

"You about done?" Not Nate, thank goodness, but Janet. "Nate has the movie ready to go."

"Uh, yes." Tessa looked down at her pruned fingers. When was the last time she'd spoiled herself with a bubble bath? Had she ever? Maybe once or twice at Jared's and never on the road with her parents. She could do this every night. Would she find out soon if they planned to let her stay?

She pushed up on the sides of the tub, but that put pressure on her ankle. Getting in hadn't been easy, but she'd done it on her own. Getting out was a different story. She needed help.

"Uh, Janet?"

"Yes dear."

"I think I need help." It pinged her dignity, but what else was she to do?

After Janet helped her from the tub, Tessa put on a flower-covered sundress she'd chosen today. By herself. What a luxury that had been! For the first time in years, when she looked in the mirror, she saw herself, not the image someone else created her to be.

If she could have skipped down the steps, she would have, but Nate waited for her at the top of the stairway.

He offered his arm, and she reluctantly took it. After tomorrow, he'd leave, and she'd get to traverse the steps on her own. As it should be.

A scent wafted toward her as she hopped down one step, and she breathed in? A woodsy scent. Cologne?

Warning bells screeched in her head. Cologne had been one of the first things that had attracted her to Jared. He'd smelled manly, like new leather. She'd learned since that the scent covered a skunk.

But Nate's woodsy scent . . . He wasn't trying to hit on her, was he? Was Caroline right?

She descended another step with Nate's strong but gentle care.

No. Nate was not like Jared. And he was only being a gentleman.

She hoped.

Still, as soon as they'd hit the floor at the bottom of the steps, she released his arm and shooed him off. If she were to truly be independent, that meant walking on her own, even if it involved crutches.

She slowly walked across the dark backyard, careful of her crutch placement on the uneven ground, and gasped. The side of the pole shed had been transformed into a movie screen, and camping chairs were set up in a couple rows for viewing: two chairs in front and four in back. Janet and Marcus were already seated, as were Debbie and some man. Her husband maybe?

On a table to the right of the screen was a massive tub of popcorn along with another tub filled with ice and pop cans. A tray of chocolate-peanut butter bars also sat on the table. This family knew how to do movies well.

When was the last time she'd had fun?

She couldn't remember, but no doubt she would remember this evening. Hopefully, the movie was as good as the setting.

She lifted a silent prayer asking that this family would decide to let her stay with them.

Nate was fiddling with the projector as she approached, and he showed her a big grin once he noticed her. Then everyone else turned around, and she felt like she was in the spotlight though it was dark outside.

They all stood, and when she arrived at the seating area, Debbie took the hand of the man beside her. "Tessa, this is my husband, Jerry. We actually get a date night tonight."

Jerry offered his hand. "Nice to meet you, Tessa. And welcome to the Brooks family."

What? Her brows furrowed, she glanced from Janet to Marcus then back at Janet.

Janet walked over to Tessa. "If you'd like to stay with us until you're healed, we'd love to have you." She held open her arms.

Tessa tensed and backed off. A hug might be a small gesture, but Tessa just couldn't do it. Would that make them change their minds about welcoming her?

"Please forgive me." Janet's hand flew to her chest. "I'm a hugger and forget others aren't the same way."

"It's okay." She couldn't believe someone not only took her feelings into consideration but also apologized for stepping over her personal boundaries.

"Yeah, watch out for Mom, the crazy hugger." Nate elbowed his mom and nodded toward a chair in the front row that had a footrest. "Special for you." He helped her sit down, then handed her a blanket and offered to get her a plate of food.

"Just warning you, our family likes butter on our popcorn. Lots of butter."

She giggled. "Guess that's a risk I'll have to take."

A minute later, he delivered a paper plate filled with popcorn and a couple of bars that had to have thousands of calories a piece. Then he set up a TV tray between his chair and hers, so she wouldn't have to hold her plate the entire time.

She couldn't help but compare Nate's behavior to Jared's.

One forced her to wait on him. The other waited on her without being asked.

And not once did Nate make her feel guilty or obligated for that service. Oh, if only she'd waited for the right man. Her hands cradled her stomach, just as a black cat jumped onto her lap.

"Falcon. Down," Nate called out.

"It's okay. I like him."

"You sure?"

She stroked his silky fur, and his purr machine started up. "It's relaxing."

"Okay then." Nate set an overfilled plate on the table between them and sat down. "Ready everyone?"

"Yep." "Go for it." "What are you waiting for?" All rang out as Nate hit a button on his remote.

Seconds later the movie began.

And a few hours later she was in love with a new man.

Captain America.

Oh, yeah. He could rescue her any time.

"Like it?" Nate picked up their empty plates and threw them in a plastic bag.

"You said there are more of these movies?"

"A whole slew of Marvel hero movies. About twenty of them out right now. I'm game to watch one or two a weekend, after Dad and I work on The Draken."

His mom followed behind him, tossing pop cans in a different bag. "I vote we watch *Thor* next week."

Nate groaned. "And watch you swoon over some over-muscled blond jerk?"

Janet leaned down and whispered to Tessa. "Worth it!"

That she had to see. "I vote we watch *Thor* next week."

"Thanks, Mom." He held his hand out to Tessa. "Help you up?"

"Did you learn your manners from Captain America?" She accepted his hand.

"Why, yes he did." Marcus chimed in from behind her. "I taught him everything he knows."

Nate stabbed a fist to his heart. "Just shoot me now. Please."

Tessa couldn't suppress a giggle that burst into a belly laugh. Nate's parents and aunt and uncle joined in the laughter. It had been so long since she'd laughed, it almost knocked her back onto her chair.

"Whoa there." Nate stretched an arm behind her back, helping her regain her balance. "No more broken limbs, got that?"

She couldn't make that promise. To be honest, she'd break every bone in her body if it meant she got to stay with this family. For the first time she could remember, she felt loved.

Problem was, love never lasted.

Chapter Ten

This coffee shop wasn't as comfortable to work in as Brandt's Burgers, but with having to take Tessa to the hospital on Friday, Nate needed to work on his side job at night this week. During the evening, Brandt's would have too many distractions, and he preferred to work away from home. Plus, he had to work on building a potential client list if he ever wanted to achieve his dream.

He scanned over the list of small companies recommended to him by Brandt and by Carter, his lawyer friend. Burke's Lawn Care. I-Spy Home Security. Vince's Vacuum Repair. J.A. Red's Computer Repair. This list was a good start. In order to make the sale, though, he needed to do his research.

But first he needed to take care of the client he already had. He opened his Mac on the two-person circular table and brought up the website he was working on for Carter who was about to open his own law office. This was Nate's first big project on his own, and he wanted to bring his A game, which meant research into boring legal stuff, which meant he needed to concentrate.

Carter had recommended several legal websites he liked, so that was where Nate started. He brought up all the sites and took notes on what he thought worked and what didn't.

The metallic tone of an electric guitar shook him from his research. He looked behind him and saw a woman setting up to play. Yay . . . He grimaced. Why hadn't he brought his earbuds?

Well, he'd just have to work through it. Maybe the music would be good and would enhance his work experience. Yeah, he'd go with that. It was all about mindset, right?

While she set up, he chose the theme he thought worked best for a legal website then added the header and logo Carter had previously approved. He tested that with a few other themes he planned to show Carter. Nate liked the first the best, but he didn't have the final say.

The musician began to play, a soulful ballad that didn't work with her guitar. Or maybe her voice didn't work. Either way, it was distracting. Now, if Tessa was up there singing, that would be a different kind of distraction.

Wait . . .

When he'd left home yesterday, Tessa had told him she felt bad for not being able to help out much. What if she could sing at that indie coffee shop in Brainerd? Mom spent half her earnings at that shop, so she could put in a good word for Tessa. And singing was something she could do with a broken ankle, as long as she had transportation to and from town.

That was the crick in this plan.

Running scenarios through his mind, he tapped his finger on the table. His mom or dad sure didn't have time. His brother Josh didn't have time. And Nate lived two-plus hours away. Given her situation, she wouldn't accept rides from just anyone, so Uber was out of the question. Maybe if she performed weekends only? He'd be up there anyway, working on The Draken. He could chauffeur her.

Yeah. That would work. He'd propose it after her surgery. That would give her a reason to keep pressing on. That would give her hope, which she desperately needed.

He stared at his computer and groaned. The more time he spent with Tessa, the less he had to work on establishing his business, and the longer it would take to hit the road in The Draken.

Whatever God was doing right now was putting a major crimp in Nate's plans. He wasn't terribly happy with the detour, but he'd learned that God's side trips always worked out for the best, so he'd follow. Probably grumbling all the way.

*

Seated by the kitchen island, Tessa peeled a carrot then cut it up into finger food strips. At least she was doing something to earn her keep here. Janet had been really good about letting Tessa help where she could. She'd even conquered going up and down the stairs by herself, so no one needed to babysit her.

After the surgery, maybe she could move back into the bus and get out of this family's way.

Surgery. Tomorrow. Being around people who genuinely seemed to care for her, the week had flown by. Actually, the day had arrived way too quickly. The surgery didn't frighten her as much as going back to the cities.

What if Jared had found out about her surgery? What if he

was at the hospital waiting for her? What would he do?

He hadn't physically hurt her. Yet. But . . .

Images of the broken crib played through her mind. What if she'd been on the end of that rage instead of the crib?

She shuddered thinking about it and whispered a prayer for God's protection. So far, this past week, He hadn't let her down.

Like a whirlwind, Janet whooshed into the kitchen as Tessa cut up the final carrot.

"Thank you for doing this." Janet gathered up the carrots along with watermelon and berries that Tessa had cut up. "You are a godsend. I never realized how much Jaclyn helped me, until she was gone."

"I can't wait to meet her."

"Sunday. And she can't wait to meet you. Ever since Lauren moved to New York, she's been moping. That child needs a big sister around."

A big sister? Tessa couldn't hold in a smile. As an only child, she'd always wanted a sibling. Now with Nate, Josh, and Jaclyn, she'd have three. Hopefully, she'd meet Lauren someday too, before she left for Auntie Shay's cabin.

She readjusted her leg on the stool beside her and patted it. Who knew a broken bone would be a blessing. God must have known she needed a family.

But would they still be family once she moved out?

Nope. Not going there. She had six more weeks of recovery before she was even supposed to put pressure on the foot. That meant a minimum of six more weeks with this family. She trusted them, had let her guard down around them, and that scared her to death. They could still turn out to be like

Jared.

Marcus strode through the kitchen, pausing for a second to grab a cookie from a plate on the island. With Janet in the baking business, this house always overflowed with sweets.

Janet rapped his hand, making the cookie fall to the floor and break.

"That was a perfectly good cookie." Marcus bent down, and Janet swatted his behind.

"And we're heading to a perfectly good supper with friends."

Blushing, Tessa looked away.

"One cookie won't hurt."

"Uh-huh." Janet patted his stomach then bent over to clean up the mess. "Remember when you were skinny?"

"I resemble that remark." He smirked.

Janet shook her head but chuckled and gave him a shove toward the mudroom that led to the garage. "Time to go, Mr. Formerly-Skinny."

And a giggle broke free from Tessa. Oh, to have that kind of relationship. Maybe someday, but she knew she had a long road to travel before she truly arrived at a place called home.

Janet looked back at Tessa. "We'll set the house alarm on the way out, so you don't need to worry. Enjoy your quiet time. Nate'll probably get in late."

"I will. You have fun too." Tonight, the couple was going to some party, and that would leave her alone, at least until Nate arrived. Then early tomorrow, he would bring her down to the cities for the surgery.

That was a whole bunch of time spent with just Nate. Goosebumps broke out on her arms and legs. Would she ever trust a man again? So far Nate hadn't given her reason for mistrust.

But then, she'd only spent a few days with him. Jared hadn't shown his true stripes for several months.

Or maybe she just hadn't noticed Jared's controlling ways immediately. She had to remain watchful, observant so she didn't fall into that trap again.

She listened to the garage door lower, and peace came over her. This was the first moment she'd truly had all to herself since Nate had picked her up.

What if Jared found her tonight before Nate got home?

Her peace instantly fled, and a chill rushed through her veins. If he found her, she'd be helpless. Was this how her life was going to be from now on? Every moment she was left alone, fear would take over?

No. She couldn't—wouldn't—live life that way.

Which meant she needed a diversion, or her evening would be spent in worry.

She grabbed her crutches and got off the stool. The laptop Nate had brought down for her remained on an end table in the family room. She sat on the couch and pulled the computer onto her lap. She raised the lid and hit the 'on' button. At least, she thought it was the 'on' button.

A bunch of stuff flashed on the screen, then after a minute or so, something appeared asking for her password. Nate had told her the password when he'd given her the laptop, but she hadn't paid attention. Why, when she knew nothing about computers? If she did understand computers, she'd search for information on her parents. So far, she hadn't gotten up the nerve to ask for help.

How did a twenty-two-year-old confess she was clueless? Her parents hadn't owned computers, and Jared—a computer engineer—had hidden his away. For her safety.

Ha! That was just one more level of control he'd exerted over her.

She closed the laptop and set it aside. This weekend, she'd ask Nate for help, then next week she'd do some research. Would her parents forgive her for running away with Jared? Would they welcome her back home, even if the place called home was a bus?

Ugh! This was why she hated being alone. Her thoughts seemed to scatter in a zillion directions, and none of those directions led to some place good.

She picked up the remote for the television and hit the power button. That button she knew was right because it was labeled 'Power." She clicked through probably a hundred channels, but nothing caught her attention. The only shows she'd watched at Jared's were the ones he'd chosen.

Another freedom she'd sacrificed. How had that happened?

If only she had a guitar or piano, singing could keep her occupied for hours. Once she got out on her own, the first thing she'd buy would be a guitar.

But did she really need an instrument?

She closed her eyes and pictured her parents onstage singing some hymn they'd modified to bluegrass sound. Sometimes Tessa would join in. Audiences had loved their music. She'd loved the lyrics but didn't like her parents' interpretation and had believed that with Jared she'd finally have the freedom to sing the music in her soul.

He wasn't stopping her anymore.

Using her crutches, she stood up and the words to "How Great Thou Art" sang from her lips. A contemporary, soulful version straight from her heart. She braced her knee on the couch cushion and let her crutches fall to the side as she spread out her arms. "It Is Well with My Soul" poured out, followed by "Amazing Grace" and more as she lost herself in musical praise, using the gift God had given her, and tears finally flowed down her face.

The putt of a vehicle coming up the driveaway barely registered in her mind as she kept singing. It had been too long. She prayed out the first line of "Be Thou My Vision" and the home alarm trilled like a police car speeding through the room.

Her scream added to the siren as her leg collapsed, and she fell face first on the couch. Her crutches lay on the floor, too far for her to grasp quickly.

Jared was coming, and she wasn't able to run from him.

Chapter Eleven

The heavenly sound of Tessa's voice was crashed by the ear-splitting home alarm. Idiot! Nate had been so caught up into listening, that he'd completely forgotten to disable the alarm before entering. Tessa had to be frightened out of her life.

He punched in the numbers, but his fingers suddenly seemed to grow fat, and he couldn't hit just one at a time. He slowed his breathing, hoping to slow the mad race of his heart, and carefully pressed the correct code.

Finally, the alarm stopped.

And silence answered.

"Tessa?" He listened and heard nothing. He stepped out of the mudroom and scanned the kitchen, the stairs, the dining room. No sign of her. He stepped further into the kitchen where he would have a view of the family room. "Tessa!"

He ran to her. She laid on the couch, her head and her upper torso covered with a blanket, but that didn't stop him from seeing her whole body quake. "I'm sorry, Tessa. I forgot to turn off the alarm." He knelt on the floor beside her and slowly pulled the blanket away from her face. It was white as a January snow, and dampened with tears. Oh, he was an idiot. "Forgive me?"

She hugged herself, but that didn't stop the shivering. "Not your fault. I'm a . . . a head case," she whimpered.

"No. You're not." He brushed hair away from her eyes. "You've been through trauma, and I just added to it. Your reaction is normal." He wasn't certain that was true, but it made sense to him, and if his words calmed her, that was all the mattered.

Keeping the blanket around her shoulders, she sat up and wiped the back of her hand across her cheeks. "When will it stop? When will I stop reacting every time someone says, 'Boo'?"

"It's been a week, Tessa. I'm no psychologist, but I'm certain your troubles don't disappear in seven days."

She drew her healthy leg to her chest and looked over it toward the kitchen. "Why are you doing this, Nate? Why is your family so nice to me?"

He shrugged. "Guess we've learned that when God places someone on our doorstep, we don't turn them away."

"You think God brought me here?"

"I don't have any other explanation. Do you? And the way you were singing a few minutes ago—"

"You could hear me?"

He nodded at the open window in the kitchen. "And I'm guilty of stopping to listen." He touched her hand. "You sing like an angel."

"You really think so?"

"I could listen forever. As a matter of fact, I was going to bring this up later this weekend, after I'd talked to Mom, but I think we can get you a gig at a coffee shop in town."

"You're joking, right? Jared always said no one would listen to me."

"Well he lied to you. Got that?" His hands balled into fists. How he wished he could punch that dude in the face. What kind of man constantly put down his girlfriend?

A smile actually snuck out on her lips. She tried hiding it by gnawing on her lip but failed. "So, you think I sing well?"

He grinned. "Never heard better." He drew an X over his heart. "I swear."

"And you really think people would listen to me?"

"Ha! They'd beg for you."

Her smile broke free, but then disappeared as fast as it had come. "There's one problem."

"We'll deal with it."

"Really? Do you have a guitar or keyboard? Does the coffee shop have a piano?"

"Oh." His nose and mouth wrinkled. "I don't think they have a piano. Lauren had one here, but that got moved to Our Home."

"Well, it was a good idea."

"Hey, I'm not giving up on it yet. Just wait, I'll come up with a solution." But first he had to make sure the coffee shop would let her sing, then he'd worry about the guitar.

After he brought her home from surgery tomorrow, he'd drag his mom into town and she'd do the convincing.

Tessa shivered as Nate drove up to the hospital. It had been a year since she'd kissed her precious Cadence goodbye, but hospitals still meant death to her.

"Scared?" Nate pulled into the patient drop-off.

"A little." Which was true, but she wasn't going to tell him the real reason she didn't want to be here.

Nate parked then came around his father's pickup—that rode far smoother than Nate's—and opened her door. He helped her out of the truck and into a wheelchair. Her gaze slid back and forth as they entered through the big revolving door. No sign of a tall, brown-haired, well-dressed man looking her way. Jared had never been able to hide, and he'd loved the attention from women.

Even a year ago, when she was in torment, he'd flirted with women.

She'd once thought she was special because he'd chosen her.

Ha. Guess the joke was on her.

Nate left her in the lobby while he parked the pickup in the ramp. Then he wheeled her up to the surgery center where she checked in, handing over her insurance card that would eventually become a breadcrumb for Jared to follow, but in the wrong direction.

She hoped.

Just as she hoped this surgery went well.

Nate's family had prayed over her this morning, and she knew they'd be praying all day. That meant something to God, right? He'd honor those prayers.

A nurse called out "Tessitura Chanson."

"Tessitura?" Nate looked at her sideways.

She rolled her eyes. "My full name."

"It's pretty." He grinned and nudged her toward the nurse.

"Can he join me?" Tessa gestured toward him.

"Until it's time for surgery."

"You sure you want me in there while they're poking and prodding you?"

She hugged herself. "I don't want to be alone."

"Then I guess I'm coming with you."

For the next two hours, he was with her while medical personnel asked a slew of questions and took her vitals and hooked her up to an IV.

Not once over that time did he make her feel worthless. Not once did he flirt with a nurse, or even with her. Was his care for her all an act? Or was he the real deal, like Caroline's husband?

"Time to go for a ride." The in-charge nurse came in and unlocked the wheels on her bed.

Tessa connected gazes with Nate. "Keep praying?"

He grinned. "I haven't stopped."

Whoo boy, if Nate wasn't careful, he'd fall for that cute, spunky, and messed-up redhead. He watched the nurses roll the bed from the curtained-off room, taking Tessa to surgery. She was facing that far better than being alone. His mom had mentioned that Bible verse about guarding his heart. She was right, especially when he somehow ended up as Tessa's caretaker.

How had it come to this, that he was spending an entire day

at the hospital with a woman he hardly knew? Usually when he dropped off people at Our Home, they would go on with their lives. Yeah, there was the guy he'd picked up outside a bar a few months back who'd become a friend, but he was the exception. For his sanity, Nate needed it to be that way.

Somehow, Tessa was different. What was God's plan in all of this? Nate sure didn't have a clue.

He slung his messenger bag over his shoulder and left Tessa's room to grab something from the cafeteria and maybe get some work done. The surgery was supposed to take a couple hours, followed by about an hour in recovery, so Nate could make a dent in his work. The nurses had his cell number to keep him apprised of what was happening, so he didn't have to worry about constantly asking for an update.

He found the cafeteria on the first level and set up his temporary office in a back corner, away from chatter. Then he ordered a breakfast platter and said grace, along with throwing in a prayer for Tessa and all the medical personnel caring for her.

After eating the tasteless breakfast—he'd be the first to admit he'd been spoiled by his mom's cooking—he opened his Mac and continued working on the website design. Carter had been pleased with what Nate had gotten done earlier in the week. Now to flesh it out. If he did a good job here and was able to get a positive reference from Carter, then he was a step closer to becoming his own boss and being free to roam the country in The Draken. Now that would be the no-strings-attached life he craved.

A couple hours later his phone buzzed, and the nurse informed him Tessa was out of surgery and that it had gone well. Now she was heading for recovery. They'd let him know when he could rejoin her then take her home.

He lifted up a silent prayer of thanks then closed his laptop. With her in recovery, there probably wasn't enough time to focus on his project. Instead he grabbed a chocolate brownie from the cafeteria, then brought up a book on his phone. A little more than an hour later, his cell phone buzzed again. He could return to Tessa's room.

Nate rode the elevator up three floors then walked past curtained rooms until he found Tessa's. Her eyes were closed, but she looked at peace.

But then her brow furrowed, and she mumbled something, "Cady."

That was what he thought she said anyway. He sat in the chair squished between the wall and her bed and touched her hand. "Hey Tessa, this is Nate."

Her eyes flickered open. She turned her head to the side and stared quizzically at him at first, but then her expression relaxed. "Nate." Her voice was hushed. "Is it done?"

"Yep. They said it all went well. You should be out of here soon."

"Oh. Good." Her eyes closed, and peace swept over her features.

Minutes later, her forehead wrinkled, and she muttered something. "Where's Cady. Is she all right?"

Who was Cady? And why hadn't Tessa mentioned her before? Not that he knew everything about Tessa, but if she was mumbling about Cady in her sleep, clearly this person was important to her.

A nurse knocked on the wall, then entered the room. "Wake

up, sleepyhead."

Tessa's eyes flickered open.

"Time to take a few more vitals."

"Is surgery done?" Tessa asked the nurse.

"Yes, and Dr. Manila will be here soon to tell you all about it."

"Thanks." Tessa yawned. "I'm tired." She closed her eyes as the nurse prodded her. Moments after the nurse left, Tessa's face wrinkled, and her breathing quickened. "Cadence? Cady?"

Nate knew Tessa shied away from touch, but he squeezed her hand to draw her attention. "Hey, Tessa, you're having a bad dream." Whoever this Cady was, she was making Tessa upset. Had the hospital triggered the memory? Or did she have these dreams every night?

Tessa's eyes fluttered open then locked with Nates'. "Oh, it's you." She looked around the room and woozily asked. "Is surgery over?"

He laughed. When he'd had his wisdom teeth pulled, apparently, he'd kept asking the same questions over and over again, too.

A few seconds later another knock sounded on the wall, and the surgeon entered the room. Nate whipped out his phone to take notes.

The doctor sat, which Nate appreciated. That put her eye to eye with both him and Tessa rather than talking down to them.

"Hello Tessa. Nate."

"Is it done?" She asked the doctor.

"All done, and you did wonderful. You'll be dancing before

you know it."

Tessa smiled. "I like to dance."

Hmm. Something else he hadn't known about her. He catalogued that tidbit of info in his brain, just in case. In case of what, he had no clue.

"Good. But that dancing will only happen if you follow instructions."

"Okay." Tessa tried to sit up, and Dr. Manila pushed a button, helping the bed rise to a sitting position. Tessa frowned. "I can't feel my leg." She lifted the cover and sighed.

"You've been given a nerve block from mid-thigh on down. Chances are you won't feel anything for a day or two."

"Oh."

"For the next week, you're wearing a splint—absolutely no putting pressure on your foot. I want to see you next Friday for your hard cast."

"Can I walk then?"

"Not yet. We'll see you three weeks later, then hopefully you'll get the cast off and you'll get a fancy boot. At that time, you can start walking without crutches. About three weeks after that, we'll remove the boot, and if you are faithful with your physical therapy, you'll be dancing again."

Tessa held out her hand and seemed to be counting on her fingers. "Seven more weeks?"

"Followed by physical therapy."

Tessa sighed. Her gaze flicked to Nate, then toward the floor, pulling her shoulders down with it. "Okay."

"No worries, Tessa." Nate nodded to her and to the surgeon. "We'll take care of you."

"Yeah." She didn't sound convinced. What was it going to

take for her to realize they weren't going to hurt her?

Dr. Manila thanked them both then left the room.

"I'm sorry." Tessa's gaze remained down. "I'm sorry I'm such a pain."

"Hey, someday you can pay it forward to someone else, right?"

"You think so?"

"No doubt." He'd learned from experience that oftentimes a word of encouragement worked better than a shove. And Tessa was definitely someone who needed encouragement.

His phone buzzed, and he pulled it from his pocket. A message from an unknown number. Probably some telemarketer or a misdial. Still, he tapped the message icon, read the text, and froze. Then read it again to make certain he'd read it correctly.

I'm here to see Tessa.

Jared? If so, how had he found out about Tessa's surgery? And how did he have Nate's number?

Chapter Twelve

*N*ate's phone buzzed again. A message from the same number.

What room are you in?

Ha! As if Nate would tell him. The question now was, how did he get Tessa out of the hospital without Jared spotting them. Assuming the text was from Jared.

"Problem?" Tessa asked.

"Um. I'm not sure. Have to talk with Dad." His heartbeat galloped as he scrolled to find his dad's number. He'd know what to do.

The phone vibrated one more time.

Oh, by the way, this is Tessa's friend Caroline.

Nate wasn't falling for that trick.

But what if this really was Caroline? Grrr. He was as bad as Tessa for jumping to conclusions. Well, there was one way to find out without concerning Tessa. He got up and threw a grin at her, so she wouldn't worry. "Be right back. Then we'll get you home."

He stepped out of the room and typed in a response to 'Caroline.'

How do I know you're not Jared?

Meet me in the hospital lobby.

What do you look like?

Tessa told me about you.
I'll find you.

Uh-uh. That's not how this works.

Fine.
I'm about Tessa's height.
Short blonde hair.
Wearing a teal top and navy shorts.

Gotcha. Be right there.
Be prepared to show I.D.

Seriously?

I'm protecting your friend.

Fine.

He pocketed his phone then stopped at the nurses station first and warned them about Jared, just in case he was trying to get Nate from the room so he could get to Tessa. Then he hurried to the elevator and down to the first floor to the lobby.

He stepped out of the elevator and looked around. Tension squeezed every muscle in his body.

"Nate?"

He whipped around.

There stood a woman just as she'd described in the texts. With one eyebrow quirked, she showed him her driver's license. "Believe me now?"

He took the license, compared the picture to the woman, and read the name before relaxing. "Nice to meet you, Caroline." He handed back the license.

"And thank you for being vigilant for Tessa."

"She's had enough to deal with without me screwing up." He led her to the elevator and hit the number 4. "Does she know you're coming?"

"I didn't know I was coming, but my husband came home from work early just for me."

"Sounds like a class act."

"He's the best." She reached out and hit the button to stop the elevator. They jerked to a stop, and he fell against the elevator wall, banging his head. "I have a few questions for you."

"Talk about being vigilant." He rubbed the back of his head.

"When you've watched your friend go through what Tessa's gone through, you'd do anything to help them."

Nate leaned against the elevator wall, crossed one ankle over the other, and stuck his hands in his front pockets. "Shoot."

"How safe is your place?"

"Safe? Well, we have a home alarm, if that's what you're talking about. My folks are both pretty handy with a hunting rifle."

"Not you?"

"Never got into hunting." Which had disappointed his dad, but Josh made up for it. That kid lived to hunt. "But that's not the point. She's safe."

"That's good, because Jared now has a gun."

"Say what?"

Caroline sighed. "He stopped by our place yesterday, just to brag about the handgun he bought. I never thought he was the type, but I don't know anymore. Tessa leaving has pushed him into new territory."

"Wonderful." Nate shoved off the wall. His balled fists wanted to punch something. Oh, Dad was not going to be happy about this revelation.

"I don't want Tessa to know."

"I agree. And you'll let me know if you see any movement on his part."

"Absolutely." She reached toward the panel.

Nate blocked it and looked down at her. "Uh-uh, now I have some questions for you."

"I guess that's fair."

"What do you know about Tessa's past? Her family?"

She crossed her arms and stared up at him, clearly not intimidated by his height. "If she wants you to know, she'll tell you."

"What about Cadence . . . Cady? Who is she? During recovery here, Tessa's been saying 'Cady' in her sleep."

"Oh, Tessa." Caroline looked down and wiped a finger over her eyes.

"What happened?"

Caroline jutted her chin upward, her red-eyed gaze shooting at him. "Why do you need to know?"

So, she was going to be stubborn. Well, he wasn't backing down. He crossed his arms and lasered a look right back at her. "Because my family's put it all on the line for Tessa. Including our safety. I think we deserve to have some questions answered."

Caroline sighed and looked down at her foot drawing an imaginary shape on the floor. "Cady was her baby girl. Tessa miscarried her about a year ago. Jerkwad . . . " She looked up at Nate, and fire blazed in her eyes. "He told her it was for the best, then a little over a week ago, he tore apart the crib. That's when Tessa left."

Nate slowly blew out his breath as he hit the elevator button. What had he gotten his family into? A guy with a gun who would tear apart a crib? No wonder Tessa was jumpy.

He looked upward and lifted a silent prayer, *God, I don't know why you put Tessa in my path, and I'm feeling I'm in way over my head. I'm really going to need your help here. Help us keep her safe. Help us to love her like you do.*

Chapter Thirteen

Tessa lay in the bed at the Brooks' home, arms barricading her stomach, her emotions as numb as her leg. Once again, she had left the hospital with empty arms, and that had brought all of it back. The painful contractions and delivery of her precious Cadence, too small at eighteen weeks to live. The callous response from Jared, telling her the miscarriage was a stroke of luck and that she should get her tubes tied.

Those had been the words that had pushed her to plan her escape, but it wasn't until he destroyed Cady's crib that she gathered the courage to follow through.

How had she once imagined him to be her white knight, rescuing her from a dull life on the road, with no real home to speak of? The man was pure evil.

A knock on the door pulled her from her wallowing. She drew blankets up to her chin. "Come in."

Janet opened the door and peeked inside. "How you doing, hon? You hungry?"

She chuckled. Nate had said his mom would bandage the hurts with food. It had always worked for him. Today, it would work for her too. She hadn't eaten for over twenty-four hours, so yeah, she was hungry. "I'm starving."

"I thought so." Janet shouldered open the door and entered with a tray of food. Sliced pork and a spinach salad flavored with strawberries, mandarin orange slices, pineapple, and walnuts. And a chocolate bar. With Janet, chocolate was a staple, not that Tessa minded.

Tessa tried sitting up.

Janet rushed over, set the food on a TV tray beside the bed, and packed pillows behind Tessa's back. "How's that?"

"Perfect." Really, it was better than perfect. She hadn't had anyone mother her in over four years, unless you counted the times Jared was apologizing.

Janet handed the tray to Tessa, then gestured to her cell phone on the nightstand. "Need anything, call."

"Uh well, actually . . . " She'd like some distraction to take her mind off Cadence. "I was wondering if Nate could bring up his old laptop." She sighed and looked out the window at the backyard where they'd watched a movie only six days ago. "And teach me."

"He'd be glad to. That boy's been pacing the house, driving me nuts, ever since he brought you home. He didn't even have seconds for supper." She squeezed Tessa's shoulder. "We're here for you."

"Thank you."

Janet left the room as Tessa sliced off a small piece of the pork, then put it into her mouth. Flavor exploded on her tongue. Oh. My. How was it some people could take something ordinary and make it taste better than anyone else? She was going to gain a ton of weight living here, especially without having use of her leg.

Maybe that was a good thing. Maybe Jared would no longer want her if she became pudgy. He'd been so strict about what she ate.

How had she allowed him to take over every facet of her life? Even now, he was constantly on her mind.

Well, he wasn't welcome to this meal. She took a bite of her salad and moaned. No dressing, but it wasn't needed, not with fresh fruit adding flavor. Feeling mischievous, she took a bite of the bar. Caramel and chocolate mixed together. Oh, yeah, she was going to gain weight and not regret a pound.

A knock sounded on the door, and Tessa dropped the bar, suddenly feeling guilty for eating dessert before the meal. She wiped her mouth with a napkin and balled the napkin up so whoever it was wouldn't see chocolate remnants. "Come on in."

As usual, Nate was smiling as he entered, laptop in hand. "Mom said you wanted this." He set it on her nightstand then sat in the chair on the other side of the bed. "How ya feeling?"

"Hungry." She forked more salad. "This is amazing."

"Right? I don't know how my mom does it. I follow her exact recipes and it tastes blah compared to Mom's."

"Some people have the gift."

He snapped his fingers. "Speaking of a gift." He held up a hand. "Don't go anywhere."

She snorted.

And he flashed that cute grin before heading out of the room.

Music swirled in her gut. Heaven help her, she was falling fast. Just like she had with Jared. Caroline had noticed the looks this afternoon and warned Tessa. Oh, her head knew what was right, but try telling that to her heart.

A few minutes, and several bites of food later, Nate came back into the room, holding something behind his back. But his skinny body was doing a poor job of hiding it.

Both hands flew to her chest where her heart took off like a polka. "A guitar?"

"Ah, you ruined my surprise." He whipped the guitar—a 12-string Ovation!—from behind his back. He cradled the fingerboard in one hand and the rounded black body in the other. It wasn't new, by any means. It didn't even have an output jack, but it was beautiful.

"May I?" She set her food on the TV tray and wiped her hands with a napkin.

"Uncle Jerry tuned it first. Said it's been sitting around their house collecting dust. It's yours, if you want it."

"No. Really?" She accepted the guitar and cradled it like a baby. "It's been years . . . " she whispered as she positioned her fingers to play a G-chord, then C, then A minor and E minor. The rich sound filled an empty hole in her body and tears almost sprouted. "Thank you," she said softly. "And thank Jerry, or rather, I'll thank him when I see him."

"He said you can thank him by practicing and then giving our family a little concert . . . when you're ready, of course."

She hugged the instrument to her body and swore her face had to be beaming brighter than a lighthouse. "I will gladly do that." She held up the guitar for him to take. "But first I need to eat, and then . . . " She nodded toward his laptop. "I have no clue how to use it. Is it safe?"

"Safe?" He took the guitar from her and leaned it against the wall.

"Yeah, you know, from bad things—pictures—popping up. From crazed guys stalking me."

He stared at her like she'd just said she was from Mars.

Exasperated, the words spilled out from her. "Jared's a computer engineer. He said that computers were dangerous. He was protecting me from porn and male stalkers and from people hacking into our accounts."

Nate's jaw grew rigid, then he combed fingers through his curly blond hair and sighed. "Yeah, that can happen, but there are also ways to protect yourself. That laptop has all the top security software. Doesn't mean bad things can't happen, but it sure does guard against it. It's just as dangerous getting into a car or walking down the street."

"Oh." She wouldn't tell him that Jared discouraged her from going anywhere alone for reasons of safety. The two-block walk to her job had been the entire reach of his leash.

He sat on the chair beside her bed. "Just be wise when you're searching, and you shouldn't run into problems."

She nibbled on her lower lip, ashamed by how naïve she was, and by how little she knew. "Will you teach me how to use it safely?"

He grinned. "Gladly."

And for the next hour or so, he sat beside her, teaching computer basics, including how to watch a movie.

The second Captain America movie, to be exact. By the end of the movie, she was still in love with the fictional character, but that wasn't what made her heart sing, rather it was the serious crush she had on the cute blond guy who'd enjoyed the movie with her. With a promise to watch the third Captain America movie tomorrow night on the lawn. Even after a tiring day filled with surgery and long car rides, she knew she'd have pleasant dreams tonight.

The gun shaking in Jared's hand pointed at her heart. Tears trekked down his face. "Why, Tessa, why did you leave? We can try for another baby. You know I can't live without you. My life is worthless without you."

Tessa backed into the headboard and pulled her covers up to her chin, but she was certain he could see her heart pumping through the blankets. "I . . . I'm sorry, Jared. I couldn't do it anymore."

He stepped closer until he was at the end of her bed. "Come home with me, Tessa. It'll be different this time. I promise."

And he'd keep good on that promise for a week, maybe a month if she was lucky, and then he'd revert to the man she'd come to despise.

"Stay with me." Suddenly, Nate stood beside Jared, pushing Jared's arm down until the gun aimed at the floor. "I'll save you." He splayed a hand over a white star on his shirt.

"No, he won't." Jared's arm sprang back up, his finger tight on the trigger. "Come with me."

"I . . . can't," she whispered.

"Then he won't have you either."

Light flashed, and pain exploded in her heart as the world went dark.

Chapter Fourteen

Tessa jerked up in bed, fighting the covers tangled around her.

Neither Jared nor Nate stood at the foot of her bed. It was a dream. Just a dream.

But why couldn't she feel her leg?

She untangled the covers enough to peek beneath them, confirming her leg was intact, but it was splinted. Memories rushed back at her. Broken ankle. Nerve block. Surgery. They'd told her she wouldn't feel her leg for one or two days.

Through it all Nate had been there. He had saved her.

Or was he encaging her just as Jared had?

No. That couldn't be right. With morning sunlight streaming through the window, she pulled herself up to a sitting position. Her gaze flitted to the guitar leaning against the wall next to her bed, then to the laptop on the bedside table, and something niggled at her, but what, she didn't know. Nate and his family had been nothing but good and generous. Still, something didn't feel right about this situation. The quicker she healed and made her way to Auntie Shay's cabin, the better.

A knock sounded on her door, and Tessa gasped.

"Are you all right, hon?" Janet.

Tessa forced out a long breath. "Yeah. Just had a nightmare."

"Would you like breakfast?"

"Not really." After that nightmare? She probably wouldn't be hungry for the rest of the day.

"Okay. Give us a call when you do get hungry."

"I will."

Footsteps faded, and silence filled the room. Her gaze returned to the laptop.

She might not be hungry for food, but she was hungry for knowledge. She pulled the computer onto her lap and turned it on, this time remembering the password. Minutes later she typed Chanson Family Gospel Singers into the search engine.

Where was her family? Why hadn't they returned her letters? Had they never forgiven her for running off with Jared? That went against everything they'd preached about in their ministry. If only they would have known that, had they shown up on his doorstep, she would have gone with them freely.

That was then, though. No longer did she desire to rejoin their life on the road, but she did want to confront them and ask them why they'd abandoned her.

Tessa spent much of the morning researching, then a good part of the afternoon watching more Marvel movies.

Hero movies. But not all the heroes were as selfless as the captain. Actually, many were arrogant, and not all were who they claimed to be.

She shut down the computer and set it on the nightstand. Was Nate who he claimed to be? Or was he another villain like

Jared, someone who claimed to save, yet did the opposite? With her leg trussed up like this, she wasn't any freer than she'd been with Jared.

Would Nate and his family take advantage of her handicap?

No. She wouldn't think that. All this time spent by herself had allowed too many destructive thoughts in. She was going to get up, make herself presentable, then join the Brooks family. Maybe watch Nate and his dad work on the bus. After practically growing up on a bus, she knew a thing or two about maintenance. Maybe she could help them.

She reached for her crutches and carefully climbed out of bed. The last thing she wanted to do was fall and injure the foot even more. She hobbled to the bathroom, looked in the mirror, and groaned. A destitute person stared back at her. Wild, uneven hair. Pale, splotchy face with too many freckles. If Nate got her a job singing at that coffee shop, she couldn't show up like this. They'd boo her out. But she also didn't have extra money to spend on a hair salon or new makeup. She had to save every penny for moving out on her own.

Maybe Janet could even out her hair. And Tessa could purchase cheap makeup until she started earning money.

She washed her face and brushed her teeth then made her way down the stairs. Janet was in the kitchen whipping up something fattening, no doubt. Nate and Marcus sat by the island eating pancakes stacked half a foot high.

"Hey, how you doing?" Nate got off his stool and offered it to Tessa.

"Good to be out of bed." She gladly accepted the stool.

"Would you care for an early supper?" Janet seemed to

read her mind and set aside her mixing bowl. "You could have pancakes, or I make a mean tuna sandwich."

"Actually, I was wondering if you had any more of that spinach salad from last night."

"I certainly do."

"I'll get it." Nate sprinted to the refrigerator. He pulled out several covered bowls and carried them to the island. "Here you go." He brought over a plate and silverware as she checked inside the bowls. Salad, strawberries, muskmelon, and watermelon. "Need anything else?" He stopped beside his mom and looked across the counter at Tessa.

"No, this is perfect. Thank you." She filled her plate, but before taking a bite, she wanted to ask that favor of Janet or she'd forget about it.

She tugged on one of her curls as tension zinged through her arms. What was so difficult about asking a question? It was only hair. She cleared her throat and looked over at Janet who'd resumed mixing ingredients in a bowl that had to be over a foot in diameter.

"Is there a problem, hon?" Janet held her spoon in the air.

Nate winked at Tessa and dipped a finger into the mixing bowl.

Janet swatted his finger before he had a chance to dig into the batter, but she didn't take her gaze off of Tessa.

"Uh, no, I just have a little favor to ask." Tessa pulled on curls on both sides of her head. "Would you—could you possibly cut my hair?"

"Cut it?" Nate wrinkled his nose. "I think it's cute that way. Don't cut it."

Anger zipped through Tessa's veins, and it came out in her

voice. "That is not your decision to make. If I want to cut my hair, I will. If I want to color it purple, you can't stop me."

"Wow. Overreact much?" He shook his head and aimed for the mudroom. "I'm gonna go pound some nails in The Draken."

"Nathan Brooks." Janet called after him, but he didn't stop.

Marcus grabbed a lemon bar. "I'll talk to him." He followed his son out the door.

Had she overreacted? He had no right to tell her what to do with her hair, but still ... She peered over at Janet and gulped. "I'm sorry I made him upset."

"Hon." Janet sighed and leaned toward Tessa. "Want to talk about it?"

Tessa shook her head. She couldn't explain the outburst herself.

Janet nodded. "I respect that." She set aside her spoon and wiped her hands on an apron tied around her waist. "I'd be glad to cut your hair." She tugged on one of her own blonde curls. "I know exactly how to deal with stubborn hair." She added, mumbling under her breath. "And stubborn boys."

"Thanks." Tessa looked down at her lap. Why did she keep causing problems? The sooner she left this place to make it on her own, the better.

Nate slammed the hammer down on a nail that wasn't completely flush with the board. Who was he to point the finger at someone for overreacting? Sheesh. What was wrong with him?

"Nathan." Dad. Just as he'd expected.

He raised a hand, signaling to his dad that he'd heard him and then turned to face his father who leaned against a wheel on their old Farmall tractor in the pole shed. Nate didn't need to hear what his dad left unspoken. "I'm heading back in to apologize. No lecture needed."

"Actually." Dad walked toward Nate. "I wasn't going to lecture. I figure you're old enough to know what to do when you make a mistake."

Nate set the hammer on his dad's work bench and waited for him to say more. If not a lecture, then he was probably going to impart some 'wisdom' that he'd given Nate a zillion times before. Maybe it would sink in this time.

"Have a seat." Dad pointed to a couple of upside down pails, and both men sat.

Nate rubbed his palms over his jeans, waiting.

"What was that about?" His dad nodded backward, toward the house.

Nate shrugged. "I overreacted for some reason."

"It's that reason I'm curious about."

"Ha. I don't even know."

"Then think about it." His dad should have gone into counseling like Aunt Debbie had.

Nate played the events of the past minutes over in his mind. She said she wanted to cut her hair. He told her not to because it was cute that way. And it was. Then she went ballistic, and he returned the volley. But why?

"Do you like her?"

Nate startled. Brows furrowed, he looked at his dad,

ignoring the stirring in his gut. "Sure. She's cute. A little quirky. Sings like an angel. But she's also messed up."

"Mmmm."

"What's that supposed to mean?"

"She reminds me of someone else."

In his mind, Nate scrolled through the faces of the women he'd dated. None looked at all like Tessa. "No."

"I'm not talking looks, son."

"Oh." He paged through those faces again, this time looking at their hearts, and he finally knew who Dad was talking about. "Bridget."

His dad nodded. "You can't save them all."

Nate blinked and looked toward the raftered ceiling. "But I have to try, Dad." He sniffled and wiped the back of his hand over his nose. "I know what happens when I give up." If he hadn't given up on Bridget, if he'd called her back that week, maybe she wouldn't have returned to her dad's home, and she'd still be alive.

"*You* are not their savior, Nate. Ever since Bridget, you've been picking up every broken person you come across, and I admire you for caring, for really being God's hands and feet, but at some point, you have to let God piece those broken lives together."

"But I do. Once I drop them off at Our Home, that's it. They didn't have room for Tessa, or I would have dropped her off too."

"And what have you done since you brought her here?"

"Just treated her like you and Mom always taught me."

Dad cocked his head to the side. "Really? Giving her your old laptop. Rearranging your schedule to bring her to doctor appointments. Getting her a guitar. Planning to find her a job—"

"Okay, I get the picture. But what would you want me to do?"

"Don't ask me."

"Huh?" Yah, now Dad was talking nonsense. "Then who do I ask?"

"Think about it, son. Who is the person most impacted by your actions?"

Nate rolled his eyes. Duh. "Tessa. I never asked her, I just took control. I'm an idiot."

"Maybe." Dad quirked the lopsided smile that all Brooks men seemed to share. "But you're a big-hearted idiot."

"Thanks?" Wrinkling his nose, Nate stood. He walked past his dad and slapped his back. "Thanks for the talk. Now it's time for me to do some apologizing."

"One more thing, Nathan."

Nate stopped and heaved a loud sigh. "What now?"

"Guard your heart. I get the impression that Tessa is more than one of your rescue projects."

"Noted." Nate agreed with his dad there. Problem was, Tessa had somehow eased her way past that guard. And with her living with his parents, guarding his heart had become increasingly difficult. Guess he better put on the full armor of God.

He walked out of the shed and looked upward. "A little help, please?" With that, he strode across the lawn to the house.

Inside, his mom was sweeping up copper-colored remnants of Tessa's trim. She sat on the stool, her back to him.

He had to admit, her hair looked better, more even across the back.

Sticking his hands in his pockets, he walked around the island and connected gazes with Tessa who immediately looked toward her lap. He wanted to reach across the island and tip up her chin. Good thing his hands were tucked away. "I'm sorry about that, Tessa. My outburst was juvenile. And I have no business telling you what you should do. With anything. Forgive me?"

Her head bounced up, and their eyes locked. Her head cocked to the side as if she were debating what he'd said. "I forgive you." The words didn't come out confident, though. More like she was still pondering what he'd said.

But that wasn't his to worry about.

"So, since I'm heading back to the cities tomorrow, you still interested in catching another movie at the Brooks' sit-in movie theater?"

"The third Captain America?"

"Yep."

"I'm looking forward to it."

"Then it's a date." He grinned, then realizing what he'd said, his lips flatlined. "I mean." He cleared his throat.

"That's okay. I know what you mean." And she laughed. Crystal clear, just like her singing voice. Had that been the first time he'd heard her laugh? Maybe, maybe not. But this time, he was going to remember it.

He'd apologized. But Jared had apologized too. Frequently, and in the long run, it hadn't made any difference.

Crutches beneath her arms, Tessa stared into the closet in the bedroom she stayed in. Lauren's bedroom. Apparently, Lauren wasn't technically Nate's sister, but another person this family had taken in.

Would Tessa become a member of this family like Lauren had, or when she left, would she be forgotten?

Would Jared forget her?

If only he would!

But concern for that wasn't going to ruin her evening, not when she had a date with Captain America. She'd watched a few other Marvel movies last night and today, per Nate's recommendation, just so she wouldn't be in the dark about all the characters that would be appearing in the movie. But none of the heroes were as attractive as the captain. He was someone who could rescue her!

She chose a full-length skirt to keep her legs protected from mosquitoes, and a long-sleeved jacket to layer over a T-shirt. Then she crutched her way down the steps. No surprise, Nate was right at the bottom waiting for her, but unlike before, he didn't offer to help. Part of her was happy that he gave her independence, but another part was disappointed by the lack of chivalry she'd come to expect.

Thanks to Jared, she didn't know what behavior was good and what was bad, although she felt loved by the Brooks family, where she'd never felt loved by Jared. Was that the difference? Was their faith, the belief in Jesus that she'd grown up with but abandoned, was that the difference?

She shook her head and realized Nate had already left the

house. Too much thinking right now. Just go out and enjoy the evening.

Once outside, she limped across the lawn. Only one row of chairs was set up facing the screen. Janet and Marcus were setting out popcorn and munchies on the table. She could practically feel the pounds glomming onto her body, especially as long as she couldn't bear weight on her foot. One more week until she got a cast, then three more until the boot. Then she'd be able to walk and hopefully shave off any weight she was certain to gain.

While Nate tinkered with the projector, Tessa came around the row of chairs and lowered herself into the chair with the footrest. Seconds later, Falcon leaped onto her lap and began purring while it kneaded her dress then curled into a circle.

"You're spoiling that cat." Nate grinned while angling the projector so the light was centered. "Everyone ready?"

"Show time." Marcus held Janet's hand as she sat, then he covered her with a blanket and handed her a tray of food. Was that chivalry?

Nate clicked the remote and the pre-movie ads began. "Can I get you anything?" He looked at her. "Blanket? Popcorn? Beverage? Bars?"

"Thank you for asking." It was a small thing, but it touched her that he didn't just assume or force something on her. "I'll take the blanket, a small bowl of popcorn, and a bottle of water."

"Coming right up." At the food table, he scooped popcorn into a bowl then turned back to her. "Butter? Salt?"

"No butter, and just a small amount of salt."

"No butter? But how can—" He shook his head. "Coming

right up." He carried a tray with her food behind the row of chairs. "On your left," he said then set the tray on a table beside her chair. "Anything else?"

"Oh, I think that should cover it for now." She smiled at him as he walked in front of her to his chair, and he grinned back.

Traitorous butterflies took flight in her stomach. It was far too soon to be attracted to another guy.

Haunting music played from the speakers, drawing her attention to the screen, and a second later she was hooked on the movie.

Two and a half hours later, emptiness filled her.

"What'd you think?" Nate turned to her, his eyes shining with excitement.

But she couldn't look at him. Captain America was flawed. "He's not the savior he was in the first movies."

"Savior?" Nate sat back in his chair, his nose wrinkled.

"Oh, this sounds like an excellent discussion." Janet picked up Tessa's tray. "Mind if Marcus and I join in?"

Tessa kept her gaze down. "I guess."

Seconds later, Marcus and Janet had positioned their chairs across from her and Nate.

"I'm curious"—Janet folded her hands in her blanketed lap—"about you using the term 'savior'."

Tessa shrugged. "In the first two movies, that's what he did. He saved people."

"He saved people in *Civil War* too," Nate said.

"Yes, but it cost too much. And decisions he made damaged relationships with friends. He could have made better choices."

"You're right." Marcus joined in. "I think this movie showed the humanity of the captain."

She half grinned, agreeing with Marcus. "But I didn't want him to be human. I wanted him to be better than that."

"But there's only one real Savior." Nate leaned toward her. "Cap couldn't be perfect, but Jesus is."

Tessa scraped at non-existent dirt on her fingers. "That's what I was taught growing up."

"It's the truth, Tessa." Janet reached over and took one of Tessa's hands. "Whenever we put someone other than Jesus on that savior pedestal, they can't help but fall off. Jesus was the only perfect human to ever live, and he was fully human and fully God."

She tugged her tingling hand away. Maybe that had been her problem all along. When she'd set Jared up on the pedestal, that had automatically knocked Jesus off in her mind. Even if Jared had been kinder, he never could have lived up to her expectations.

Just as Captain America couldn't.

And Nate couldn't.

Maybe it was time she opened that Bible Caroline had given her and rediscover a God who really could save her.

Chapter Fifteen

Water bottle in hand, Nate stepped out on the balcony of the condo he housesat for his aunt and uncle. The Mississippi River hummed with boat traffic, even as the sun set, and the walking path to the east of the river was full with walkers, joggers, and bicyclists all taking advantage of the warm days before winter hit. Granted, the first snowfall was still probably two-plus months away, but when the state you lived in usually had only six months—often fewer than that—without snow, you took advantage of every warm second.

He sat in one of the deck chairs and looked up at the blue sky just beginning to dim as the sun descended behind his home. Even with all the bustling going on below, this was always the best place to chat with God while in the city.

"I don't get it." He spoke out loud as he searched the clouds, hoping for some kind of visual response. His dad had reminded him to guard his heart. "How do I do that?" he asked. And listened. All he heard were the rumble of boat motors, conversations from travelers, and the chatter of birds.

He sighed. "Why do I care so much? Why her?" He took a long sip of his water and whispered, "Is it because of Bridget?"

Bridget. He heaved out a sigh that made a jogger look up at him. Bridget was the first person he'd ever brought to Our Home. Another hitchhiker with an angelic voice, who he'd cared far too much for. She'd been running from an abusive father and had seemed to be doing well at Our Home.

If only she hadn't listened to her father's promises that he'd changed. If only she'd heeded Nate's or the counselor's pleas to stay away. Near the end, in a fit of frustration, Nate had told her to go back, if that was what she wanted. He didn't care. Which had been a whopper of a lie.

And she'd paid for her decision with her life. Didn't matter now that the father was serving life in prison.

Since then, every young woman Nate had picked up, he'd dropped off with no plans to become emotionally involved again.

Until Tessa.

What was it with his stupid heart? Why was he so attracted to broken women? He massaged the tightening muscles in the back of his neck. He didn't even want to be in a relationship, but if he did, it would be with someone who had it all together, who loved God as much if not more than he did. Someone willing to travel the country with him in The Draken. Was that too much to ask?

His phone rang out Switchfoot's "Live it Well." He pulled the phone from his back pocket. Nancy? "This is Nate."

"Hello Nate. This is Nancy from Our Home. Is this a good time to talk?"

"Sure." A perfect time, actually. It would stop this stupid ruminating.

"This Friday, a room opens up at Our Home. Is your friend

still looking?"

"This Friday, as in two days from now?"

"Correct."

Just like that, his heart fell. This wasn't the answer he wanted from God. "Uh, well, she's been staying at my folks' place."

"Nathan, that isn't a road you want to travel down."

"I know, I know, but with her broken ankle, we couldn't leave her just anywhere."

"Uh-huh." The woman was exactly like his own mom. "Then it sounds like a room opened up at the perfect time. Talk to her and let me know. But no more strays, got that?"

"Yeah, sure."

She sighed. "You've got one big heart, Nathan."

Tell him about it. He grimaced.

Nancy shared a few more details before hanging up.

So, God had been listening, and He'd given a pretty quick response. But shouldn't answers to prayer make him feel better? Probably. But his dad's advice to guard his heart had come a little too late. Nate had already become used to having Tessa at the family home, and he anticipated spending the weekend there, just to see her.

He found her name in his contacts and hit call. Maybe she'd say 'no' and want to stay on with his family.

His heart hoped so, but his head said her leaving would be for the best.

Tessa laid down three kings then put her queen in the discard pile. "I'm out." She grinned as everyone around the table groaned. Growing up, she hadn't played card games as her family thought they were evil. But games with the Brooks family had nothing to do with gambling and everything to do with competition. This family liked to win.

And she loved beating them.

Nate's little sister, Jaclyn, slapped her handful of cards onto the table. "Fifty-three points. I take back saying I wanted another big sister."

Tessa laughed.

"Got you beat, Jack-O." Josh, Nate's younger brother tossed his cards to the middle of the table and made a fake angry face at Tessa. "Seventy-one. I had two, count 'em, two wild cards in my hand. Mind you, payback is coming."

Marcus and Janet had twenty-seven and thirty-six points respectively and were equally upset as their two kids. She never knew winning would be so much fun.

A familiar orchestral tune played from somewhere as Marcus gathered the cards.

"That your phone, Tessa?" Josh helped his dad with the cards.

She blinked. Oh, yeah, the "Captain America March." She dug out her phone from her front pocket. Only four people had her cell number, and two of them were seated at the table with her.

So, was it Caroline or Nate? She squinted at the small screen on her phone.

Nate. She hit 'answer.' "Hey Nate, I'm sitting here whomping your family at Thirteen."

"I wouldn't call it whomping." Marcus began dealing the cards. "Just because your nearest opponent is a hundred points behind you. That's catchable with two rounds left."

Nate snorted, likely having heard his father. "And Dad's being his typical sore loser."

Tessa laughed. "So, his attitude isn't special for me, then."

"Nope. That's his usual." Nate cleared his throat. "Um, Tessa, I have something important to talk to you about. Could you take a break from the game for a minute?"

She glanced around the kitchen table and they all nodded. "Sure." She reached for her crutches, but Janet motioned for her to stay seated, and the family scattered throughout the house.

"What's up?" she asked once everyone was out of earshot.

"I got a call from Our Home. They're gonna have an opening this coming Friday, two days from now. You could move in after your doctor appointment."

"Oh." She slumped. Was he trying to get rid of her? "And you want me to go."

"No!" He cleared his throat. "I mean, it's not up to me. This is your decision alone. If you want to go, we'll get you there. I can't think of a better place for you. That is, other than my folks', if you want to stay there."

Tessa sighed and looked around the house, a place that in this short while, had become a house she could easily call 'home' with a mother and father and siblings who loved her.

But it would never be her home. She'd never really be part of their family. Maybe it would be best to make a break now before she became even more attached. Her freedom was dependent upon reaching her aunt's cabin.

And what about her ankle? "What about doctor appointments? How will I get there?"

"They have transportation."

"Oh, okay." She nibbled on her lip.

"And FYI, there are a few requirements of living at Our Home. It doesn't cost anything to stay there. Room and board are provided, but hurt ankle or not, you have to participate in house activities and chores and service projects. You have to have a job or be actively looking for one."

All of which would be challenging, but not impossible. Actually, the requirements would probably help her in the long run, give her training she'd never had. "Can I think about it?"

"Of course. Pray about it too. I will be. But don't wait too long. The rooms never stay vacant for long. God always leads someone new to Our Home."

"I won't."

Nate gave her Nancy's phone number, and they chatted a few more minutes before saying goodbye.

Now, what did she do?

"Everything okay, hon?" Janet peeked into the kitchen from the basement.

Tessa waved her in, and Janet joined her at the table.

"There's an opening at Our Home." Tessa watched Janet's face, trying to get a read on what she was thinking, but the woman could make a living at poker. Tessa relayed what Nate had told her, and still no change in Janet's expression. Okay, then, she'd come right out and ask. "Do you want me to leave?"

Janet's brows shot up. Finally, some reaction. "Oh, hon, no.

We love having you here, but the decision isn't up to us. If you want to stay here, you are very welcome. Jaclyn's already claimed you as a big sister, and I'm rather pleased to have another daughter, but the choice isn't mine to make. Our Home is an excellent place to live and learn about life and family. Marcus and I are on the board as well as much of the Brooks family. If you choose to go there, we'll be very happy for you. If what you desire for long term is independence, they'll teach you to stand on your own."

Tessa looked down at the table covered with scattered cards. "If I go, can we stay in touch?"

"I wouldn't have it any other way."

Independence. Tessa breathed in the sweetness of that word. As much as she'd come to adore this family, she was liking Nate too much and was becoming too dependent upon him. Making a break now would be for the best. But—she peered through her lashes at Janet—having a mother again, a father, had filled an empty place in her heart she hadn't realized was there.

Tessa took several deep breaths and ruminated on her decision.

She knew what she had to do.

Chapter Sixteen

*M*idnight already. Nate had hoped Tessa would call back tonight with her decision, but he couldn't wait up anymore, not with a ten-hour day ahead of him tomorrow. He loved having Fridays off, but four ten-hour days could be killers. It would be worth it, though, if he drew in more clients. He couldn't wait to be his own boss and take on the projects he chose.

And, of course, travel the country in his bus.

That always made him smile.

Now he'd have sweet dreams. He pulled the covers up to his neck.

And the Marvel theme played on his phone. Tessa's ring.

Now she called?

He grabbed his phone from the nightstand and swiped to answer. "Hey, Tessa."

"Nate."

Uh-oh. He didn't like the sound of that. He sat up and reclined against the walnut headboard. "You made a decision."

He heard her take a deep breath and slowly blow it out. "I've talked with Nancy. On Friday I'm moving into Our Home."

"Good for you." He tried sounding upbeat, wanting to support her. Hopefully, the right tone came across. "You want me to drop you off there after your doctor appointment?"

"About that . . . "

Another uh-oh. "You don't plan to miss it, do you? The hard cast will be a lot better for you than the splint."

"It's not that. I'll get the cast, but your mom is taking me."

"Did you tell her, I planned to take you. I've got the day off."

"She knows. I asked her to take me."

"What?"

"I'm scared, Nate. You're a great guy, and that's the problem. Jared was a great guy too at first, and then . . . "

"I'm not Jared."

"But do I really know that? Since you picked me up, you've done everything for me. I haven't had to think. Haven't had to make a decision until now. I can't travel that road again. I can't risk it. It's best we make a clean break right now. After tonight, I won't call you. You shouldn't call me."

Nate wiped a hand across his nose. This was where he manned up and told her he understood and wished her well, but the words just wouldn't leave his mouth.

"I've upset you."

"No, it's just that . . . " He sighed. Did they have a good thing going? After a few weeks of knowing each other? Hardly. And really, she was giving him just want he wanted: the no-strings-attached lifestyle that would allow him to become his own boss.

Tonight, though, that sounded awfully lonely.

"I wish you well, Tessa. You're gonna do great things, I know it." There, he'd done the grown-up thing. Why did it have to hurt so badly?

With a hard cast on her foot, Tessa used her crutches to climb the steps to Our Home. Her new home. She raised her hand to knock on the door, and it flew open.

"Tessa." Nancy, whom Tessa had met briefly when Nate brought her here a few weeks back, answered the door. "Please, come on in." The woman, probably in her 50s, waved her and Janet in. She gave Janet a hug and shook Tessa's hand. Maybe someday Tessa would learn to like hugs, but in the meantime, she was pleased that Nancy respected her boundaries.

"I'll show you to your room." Nancy motioned to a staircase leading to a second floor.

"And I'll wait for you down here," Janet said.

Nancy led the way upstairs. No apologies for making her crutch her way up. No offers to help. No pity.

Tessa liked her.

At the top of the steps, Nancy gestured to the right.

"On your right is Rachel's room. At the end is where our onsite counselor stays. I believe you met Kathy."

"I did." Tessa wouldn't forget the woman who'd been right about having a doctor check out her ankle.

Nancy led her to the left. They stopped at a closed door on the right that had the word Miracle stenciled above it. "This is Keisha's room. She and Rachel and all the other residents are offsite doing a service project today. You'll meet most of the family tonight."

Family. Was that what Our Home was all about?

The next door to the right was open, showcasing a large bathroom with a shower, tub, toilet, and two other doors. "You'll share this with Keisha and Rachel." Nancy gestured to a wicker basket on the counter that held basic toiletries like toothbrush, toothpaste, soap, hair products, and more. That's your starter batch. After this, it's up to you to purchase your own."

"Wow. Thank you." She'd brought her toothbrush from the Brooks home, but that was all, so that basket of toiletries was a wonderful blessing. Yes, she still had the money she'd stashed in her pads, and the cash Caroline had hidden in her Bible, but she wanted to save that for when she moved to the cabin.

Nancy led her to the next door. "This is your room." Nancy opened the door labeled Future. Somehow, that gave Tessa hope that she would have a future beyond Jared, beyond the Brooks' house, beyond Our Home.

The room held only a queen-size bed and a dresser.

And on the bed were six bundles of bedding, with sets of towels on top of each.

"You may pick one set. It's yours to keep."

"Really? Thank you." Something she got to choose on her own. And keep! If she were a hugger, she'd have wrapped Nancy in a bear hug for this.

"Usually we have our new residents go to the storage room in the basement to choose their bedding, but with your ankle, we're letting that rule slide. I figure you'll have enough stair travel today."

"Thank you." Tessa felt like she was a broken record, but what do you tell someone who welcomes you into their home and gives you everything you need? Tessa studied each bedding set. One was pink and very lacy. She was girly, but not that much. Another set was all green. That was boring. Some had bold patterns, others subtle. Something for every taste.

She chose a plum set. This comforter had diamond tufts all over it, and it came with complementary plum and grey pillows and pillowcases. The towel set was also plum and grey. A touch of girl and a whole bunch of sophistication. Jared would never have chosen a set like this, it had too much color.

And this was all hers.

"I'll have you make your bed later, but for now, I'll give you the tour of the house."

On the main floor, Nancy showed her a kitchen large enough for a huge family and a living room with a beautiful piano she itched to sit at.

Tessa walked over to the piano and stared down at the keys. "Will I have permission to play?"

"You're a pianist? Wonderful!" Nancy clapped her hands together. "Absolutely, you may play. It's been a while since we've had a musician in the house."

Nancy also pointed out a bathroom and the office.

The basement had two bedrooms for two male residents who also shared a bathroom. The family room had a big-screen TV and reclining chairs angled to watch it, a foosball table, and another table with chairs circling it.

She followed Nancy back up the stairs but was going slower now. This hard cast wasn't a light thing to carry around, and already her leg itched like crazy. But she didn't dare complain and run the risk of getting kicked out.

Nancy awaited Tessa at the top of the stairs. "The tour's almost done. Then we'll make sure you sit and elevate your foot." They returned to the kitchen and Nancy removed a clipboard from the end of a cabinet. The top sheet had a checklist showing residents' duties for the week. "These rotate every week. Today, you get a free day, but tomorrow, you have kitchen duty. And to find out exactly what that means—" Nancy paged through the sheets on the clipboard—"you check this." The list outlined duties to complete every day, such as dishes and counter cleanup, and then once a week or as-needed jobs such as wiping down walls and appliances, mopping floors and cleaning out the fridge.

Every duty list was equally as detailed. Oh boy, living here was going to be an educational experience, that was for sure.

Then Nancy led her through the mudroom and out into what Tessa had assumed was a three-car garage. Instead, the space was divided into different areas: auto, art, woodworking, and more. "We have volunteers who come in to train residents in different skills. The goal is, when you leave here, for you to have a well-rounded skill set. We also have tutors for those needing to obtain their GED. Is that something you desire?"

"I graduated." Growing up on the road, she'd been homeschooled, but she had the diploma—actually, no she didn't. The diploma was in a keepsake box somewhere on her parents' bus.

"Very good. Our Home also has volunteers to help with college and trade school applications and financial aid, if that's your goal."

It had been once, but now . . . " I don't know what I'm

139

meant to do."

"That's okay, Tessa." Nancy smiled. "That's something you'll figure out. God has a way of bringing our gifts to light."

She sure hoped so.

Tessa followed Nancy past a dining room table with ten chairs surrounding it. Even so, it appeared those sitting would have plenty of elbow room. Nancy led her out a patio door onto a deck that had another enormous table. Janet was seated on a patio chair, reading. So, the woman did sit still.

The backyard was hemmed in with trees, but still looked large enough to play games. To her right was a garden, filled with rows of sweetcorn and pumpkins and more, that spanned the length of the backyard.

"It's sweetcorn season, isn't it?" Jared loved sweetcorn, so they had it often in August and September. One of the positive memories with him.

"Yes, it is. It's on the menu for tomorrow night."

"I can't wait."

"Have a seat." Nancy gestured to the table.

Tessa gladly obeyed and lifted her broken ankle onto a nearby chair.

Nancy sat across from her, folding her hands on top of a manila folder already on the table. "Living here is free—as in money—for you and is completely voluntary. If you want to move out, you're free to do so at any time. But if you choose to stay, Our Home has some basic ground rules that will be followed. Disobeying them can be grounds for dismissal."

Nancy opened the folder and began citing house rules such as no alcohol consumption, no having boy- or girlfriends stay overnight. Besides household duties, all residents must either have a job or be actively seeking employment. All residents were required to participate in one service project a month. Bible studies were held every morning, but attending wasn't mandatory. And more. The purpose was to prepare each resident for living on their own, and the ultimate goal of Our Home was to send capable, independent young adults out into the world where they could thrive.

Tessa was a long way from that. "How long are people usually here?"

"There is no usual. Every person who comes here is on a different journey. Some have life experiences and skills that help them move on quickly, while others have very few skills. And then it depends upon your determination. Natalie, the woman who was in the Future room before you, was here almost two years. She came in having few skills and little self-esteem. She left with a very nice college scholarship and a goal to be a veterinarian. Then Jet, a friend of Nate's, was here a little over a month before he moved on to an internship and trade school. It's really up to you."

Up to her. Not Jared. Not Nate. Just her. Broken ankle and all, she couldn't wait to begin learning.

Seated in his booth at Brandt's Burgers, Nate closed his laptop and his eyes. By now, Tessa was probably at Our Home, getting the tour. Why had she asked him to leave her alone?

Why did that matter so much to him?

Grrr. He slipped his Mac into his messenger bag. Time to

head up to his folks' and start pounding nails in The Draken. It probably only needed another couple of days to complete the interior work. Then he could travel.

Well, once his subcontracting work got him enough jobs, that is. Earlier today, he'd scheduled a meeting with J.A. Red's Computer Repair, a potential client, for next week. That would give him two, then he'd need a handful more to feel comfortable enough to quit his full-time job.

"Leaving so soon?" Werner Brandt called from behind the bar. "It's barely noon."

Nate shrugged. "Just can't focus today."

"Come belly up, let's have a talk." Werner motioned for him to come to the bar.

Uh-oh. Nate had heard that line before. Werner always said that right before beginning one of his 'counseling' sessions.

"What's bugging you, boy?" Werner asked while wiping down the countertop.

Nate lay his messenger bag on the stool beside him. "Just life."

"And does that life include a young woman?"

Nate snorted. "Of course." He knew better than to deny it. Werner would drag it out of him eventually, might as well get it out now.

Werner set a glass of Coke in front of Nate. "What is the problem, lad?"

"Someone I picked up. She was hitchhiking."

"And you saved her."

"Well, actually, my stopping for her made her run and break her ankle, so I'm not much of a savior."

"Aye, that would be a problem. And let me guess, she was

running from a man."

Nate snorted. "Yep."

"Abusive?"

"I guess he never hit her, but he was controlling."

"That's still abuse."

"And because of it, she doesn't trust me." Nate took a long draw of his Coke.

"That's not unusual, lad." Werner braced both hands on the counter. "My ex swore off men after what I did to her, so now because of what I did, my kids are growing up without any male influence in their life." He shook his head.

"But you get visitation now."

Werner nodded. "It's supervised, but yes, I see them."

"Tessa doesn't even want to see me. I mean, we weren't in a relationship, not this early, but . . . "

"But you hoped something might come of it."

Nate shrugged. "I don't know. She's messed up, but she also made me smile. I enjoyed being with her."

"Give it time, lad. Give her space to learn who she is apart from her abuser. Just know that could take a while. If she's worth it, you'll wait."

"I don't know if she is. Not yet."

"Then I guess that's something you'll have to pray about. Isn't that what you taught me?"

Nate shook his head but smiled. "It's not fair giving me my own advice." He grabbed his messenger bag,

"It's quite fair." Werner laughed as Nate got off his stool. "But before you go, I have another bit of news for you."

Nate looked back at the man who'd become a mentor.

"I've sold this place."

"No . . . " Nate knew it was coming, but this fast?

"No worries. Your corner booth is still yours. Was written into the contract. The buyer's turning my bar into one of those frou-frou craft beer places." He shook his head. "What's wrong with a plain ol' beer, nowadays?"

"That's what my dad says. But the taprooms have become big. I'm sure it'll be a hit for the new owner."

"Aye. She already has a successful taproom in Amery. But the woman has one condition on you keeping your corner booth."

Naturally. Nate leaned against the bar. "What is it?"

"A ten-percent discount on graphic services for this place, and if you're good enough, which I swore to her you are, she'll hire you for her Amery business too. Probably give you a free booth there as well."

"Really?" Nate felt the side of his mouth curl up. Maybe life on the road was closer than he'd dreamed possible. "But what will you do?"

"Bought myself a little burger joint up north. Figure the locals won't mind if I ad brats and sauerkraut to the menu." Werner tapped his chin. "Come to think of it, I'm going to be needing a graphic designer myself."

"For you, I'll do it free."

"*Nein*. You'll be paid, lad. Now get outta here. Go work on that bus of yours."

"Thanks, Werner. For everything."

Nate left the building, whistling. Who cared if he was off key? Somehow, Werner always made the day brighter. He'd go up to his folks' place and work on The Draken with his dad, finally get that all important father-son time in.

Two-plus hours later, he arrived at his parents' home, without a single temptation to stop and pick up someone. He'd change his clothes and grab a bite to eat before heading to the bus.

In Josh's room—the room Nate had once shared with his younger brother—Nate put on an old pair of jeans and a T-shirt he kept there, then hustled out of the room.

Directly across the hallway, Tessa's—Lauren's—bedroom door was open, and it drew him in.

And his stomach clenched.

All signs of Tessa were gone.

All but the guitar and his laptop.

Chapter Seventeen

*H*er foot now out of the cast and in a boot, Tessa sat beside the piano bench, instructing her latest student. Who knew she had the temperament to teach? Who knew she'd love to see her student's eyes light up when they played through a song for the first time? Five weeks at Our Home had taught her so much.

She cringed inwardly as Lavonna repeatedly hit the wrong keys, but she kept her smile as she instructed. "Just slow down, you'll get it. You're doing fine."

Nancy had said God would bring her gifts to light.

Tessa hadn't imagined God would work this fast.

Her student slowed her tempo and finished her piece.

"Well done. Now for next week, we're going to try something a bit harder."

The student's eyes widened in fear, but Tessa knew Lavonna would rise to the challenge. Tessa gave her a music theory assignment as well, and her student left. Now she had a half hour to herself before the second student arrived, and she couldn't be more excited.

She picked up the used Seagull acoustic guitar she'd found at a music store in the Twin Cities. This beauty had cost her every penny she owned, including the money she'd saved in her box of pads, and the money Caroline had given her.

Why had she left the Ovation back at the Brooks' home?

Stupid pride, that was all. She'd learned a whole bunch about pride while living at Our Home. She hadn't figured a homeless person would have any pride, but she'd quickly learned otherwise.

Well, with giving piano, guitar, and voice lessons, she'd quickly recoup her investment then start saving again.

For college.

She couldn't wait to become a full-time teacher!

But college cost money, and lessons wouldn't bring in enough, especially when she moved out on her own.

She took her guitar and plucked out an upbeat, happy version of "It is Well." The second time through, she closed her eyes, added her voice to the song, and got lost in the lyrics. She strummed the final cord, and clapping sounded in front of her.

Startled, she opened her eyes to see Nancy and several of Our Home's residents standing around her.

"That was amazing!" Keisha spread both hands over her heart.

Others wiped tears from their eyes.

"Have you thought of going into Amery, to see if anyone would like live music?" Nancy asked.

"Uh . . . " Yes, she had. But it had been Nate's idea not hers, and once again pride had held her back. It was time to banish that word for good. "Do you think someone would want me?"

Nancy shrugged. "You won't know unless you ask."

Tessa studied the group. Four other Our Home residents,

Nancy, the counselor Kathy, and a handful of volunteers. They'd all been super supportive of her. But would one of these people she'd come to know over the past five weeks go one step further? "Um, then I need a ride into town."

A bunch of hands went up, including Keisha's. She'd recently purchased an old clunker and had worked with the volunteer mechanic to get it in drivable condition. It wasn't pretty, but it would get her from Point A to Point B safely, and Keisha loved the independence.

"I'll take ya. Just name the time."

They agreed on a time later in the week, so Tessa could put together a résumé and playlist. Maybe The Chanson Family Singers name would come in handy. Rachel helped Tessa put together an outfit that would create the brand for Tessa, including recommending her stage name be her birth name, "Tessitura."

Three days later, Tessa stood in front of the mirror in Rachel's room in a vibrantly-colored, patterned skirt that flared out, ending just above her knees, and a dark blue, loose-fitting shirt with puffy sleeves and a wide, rounded neckline. Gold flats and dangly, gold earrings completed the outfit.

She felt pretty. And for the first time she could remember, she saw herself in the mirror, not an image of who someone else wanted her to be. This Bohemian look fit her and her music style perfectly. She couldn't wait to hit Main Street today. Someone had to want free music, right? To start out, she'd play for tips. How could they turn her down?

"You look amazing, Tessitura." Rachel snuck in behind her and looked over her shoulder into the mirror. "And when they hear you sing, they won't be able to resist you."

"You really think so?" Gnawing on her lower lip, she turned around. "Singing for Our Home is one thing, but for the public? All I have are old hymns."

"That when you sing them, don't sound old at all. And I've heard you working on your own music, too."

Tessa's brows shot up. No one was supposed to hear that. Those passionate lyrics and melodies spilling out her fears and doubts were supposed to be between her and God alone.

"Don't worry. I won't tell, but I think you should share them. People can relate."

Maybe. But for now, she'd stick with the beloved, time-proven lyrics.

"Ready, Tess?" Keisha stuck her head in the room. "You look fab! Let's go get you a singing gig."

It took less than ten minutes to get to town, just enough time to make Tessa nervous. Who was she anyway to think people would want to listen to her sing? Yeah, they'd come to hear her parents sing, and sometimes she joined them, but that was different. That was a ministry. This was . . .

A dream.

And a potential future.

Guitar slung across her back, Tessa limped down the sidewalk beside Keisha. Walking without the crutches was certainly easier, but this bulky boot wasn't much better. Maybe business owners would take pity on her? Would she even want that?

"Here's stop A." Keisha, a map in her hand, highlighting all their stops today, pointed to the coffee shop. Certainly, Holy Grounds would appreciate her music. "I'll wait out here. You can win them over. You've got this, Tess."

Tessa drew in a breath then raised her chin and shoulders as Keisha opened the door. The scent of coffee flew at her, and her nose wrinkled. Oh, how could people stand to drink that nasty stuff, much less smell it? But if she got a gig here, she'd have to get used to it, starting right now.

Shoving down her insecurities, she approached the counter and asked to speak to the manager.

Without saying anything, the teenager manning the bar swept into the back room. Seconds later, she returned with a Mrs. Claus-looking woman. Just the type of person who should appreciate Tessa's music.

The woman smiled at Tessa. "Can I help you?"

Tessa forged her own smile. "I'm Tessitura, and I'm looking for a place to play." She handed the owner her résumé and playlist, then nodded to a table in a far corner. I'd be glad to provide live music for free, accepting tips only."

The manager looked over the materials Tessa had given her, and the kindly face slowly disappeared. "I'm sorry, but our clientele comes from diverse religious backgrounds, including none at all. This wouldn't work here. I wish you luck."

"Thank you anyway." Tessa faked another smile then fled the shop.

"Well? How'd it . . ." Keisha stopped midsentence as Tessa rolled her eyes.

"Too religious."

"At Holy Grounds? Well then they better give themselves a new name." With each word, she drew a line across her body with her finger. "Their loss." Keisha Xd out the business on her map and pointed to another spot. "This little café has to love you."

But Peggy's Pizza and Pie said they didn't have any room, although they had a built-in stage.

Rhonda's Sweet-tisserie really didn't have room.

Smily's Bar smelled like cigarettes.

And so on.

"One more place to try." Keisha pointed to a business off Main Street. "It's new, I think. One of those brewpubs that are popping up everywhere."

Wrinkling her nose, Tessa swung her guitar around to the front and plopped down on a metal slatted bench, taking pressure off her foot. This was the most she'd walked since running from Jared. She'd honestly thought someone would want her. She couldn't handle one more rejection. And besides, did she really want to sing in a bar?

"Won't that be going against Our Home's rules somehow? We're not allowed to drink."

"Yeah? So? No one's making you drink. You'd just be singing. Besides, I know a lot of people who go to those places just to hear music."

"Then they probably already have someone in place."

"Are you going to walk there, or do I have to drag you?"

"Fine." Tessa stood up, and her foot throbbed. "Let's do it. But then that's it for the day."

"Just this one."

Tessa limped behind Keisha. By the time they arrived at the pub, she'd be sore and sweaty on top of cranky. They traversed the final half block, and Tessa's leg begged her to sit.

"Here we are." Keisha opened the door and forcefully whispered. "Put on that smile, and win 'em over."

"Yes, ma'am." Tessa turned on that smile again and strode into the pub. Even in mid-afternoon, this place buzzed with business. She walked up to the bar, to the young woman working, and made her smile bigger. "May I speak with the manager?"

The woman smiled back. "You're speaking to her." She offered her hand. "I'm Candy."

"Tessitura." Tessa shook her hand then handed Candy her paperwork. "I'm looking for a place to sing, for tips only."

The woman studied the résumé and playlist, then appraised her with her eyes, her gaze ending on her booted foot. "Have a seat and play something for me."

"Really?" The surprise snuck out. "I'd be glad to."

She plucked out the intro to "Amazing Grace" then started to sing, losing herself in the lyrics, "I once was lost, but now I'm found. Was blind, but now I see." She sang through two verses before putting aside her guitar.

Applause rang out from the patrons. That was good, right?

Holding her breath, she looked up toward Candy.

Were those tears in her eyes?

Candy fluttered fingers in front of her face. "That was amazing. I love your interpretation."

"Really?" Her insecurity snuck out again. "Um, thank you."

Candy pulled up a chair beside her. "Tessitura . . . "

"Just call me Tessa."

"Tessa. Thank you for singing. I remember hearing The Chanson Family Singers at my church years ago, but that was quite a different sound from yours."

Tessa grimaced. "I'm just not a bluegrass fan."

"Oh, me neither, so I was very pleased to hear you going in

a completely different direction. I loved it."

"You did?" She might not be crazy about singing in a pub, but it would be a start.

Candy held up her hand. "But I don't have openings right now for new musicians."

"Oh." Tessa tried to smile but could no longer fake it, dragging her gaze down as well.

"But."

Another 'but'? Tessa looked back up.

"A friend of mine is opening a new business in town, and he's looking for musicians." Candy took out a business card and handed it to Tessa. "Tell Ben I sent you. Or, one second." Candy took out her phone. "Let's make a videocall. If he answers, you can audition right now."

Now? Tension shot through her veins. But Keisha would ream her out if she didn't audition.

Candy made the call, and seconds later Tessa repeated her version of "Amazing Grace." He asked for more and she sang, "Be Thou My Vision" followed by "In the Garden."

"So, Ben, what do you think?" Candy winked at Tessa.

"I think I found myself a musician."

Chapter Eighteen

Nate dipped a rag into the stain, then wiped the rag over one last unstained part of his kitchen cabinet. The last unfinished part of The Draken. Too bad Tessa wasn't here to see it. Had it really been six weeks since she'd left?

She would have gotten rid of the cast a while ago. Did she still wear the boot?

And why was he still thinking about her?

Shaking off her image, he stepped back and looked at his handiwork, and tears almost leaked from his eyes.

"Good job." His dad patted him on the back.

Nothing was sweeter than praise from this man who made a living building homes and had a stellar reputation as a quality builder. On top of being an amazing dad.

Nate was blessed. "Thanks."

"Now what?" His dad plopped into the captain's chair near the front of the bus.

"Now I keep building my business, and pretty soon I'll be living on the road." Since Tessa left, he'd signed J.A. Red's Computer Repair, Up North Brewing Co., and I-Spy Home Security, plus he had a few more businesses he planned to contact, including one he was checking out tonight. Before he knew it, he'd be on his own!

"You do great work. And that dragon painted on the outside of Draken is about the best advertising you have."

"I agree." He checked his watch. "Only an hour before I have to head back to the cities, and I've got to shower first."

Dad rubbed a finger beneath his nose. "Good plan."

"Ha ha. Aren't you the funny guy?" Nate capped the can of stain and threw the rag into a garbage bag.

"What's going on in the cities?" Dad led the way out of the bus.

"The woman who bought Brandt's recommended my design services to a friend. I want to check out the place before I write up a proposal."

"Smart."

"I hope so."

Three hours later, Nate walked into Roasted to a Tea, an old bar renovated as a coffee and tea shop. The place was as busy as the brewpub he did graphic design for but had even more atmosphere. It had tin ceilings and a live-edge wood bar that had recently been varnished, sealing in a history of water rings, knicks, and what was likely cigarette burns. Toward the back of the room was what looked like a mini stage. Hopefully, he'd hear some music tonight. That would help in crafting his design.

He spotted a couple leaving a few tables away from the stage, so he squeezed past the crowded bar and grabbed the table that had a single yellow flower in a glass vase in the center. From here he had a perfect view of the place. He snapped photos with his phone and took notes: unique selection of coffees and teas, including original recipes. Pastries provided by a local bakery. An outside patio with a handful of metal tables and chairs, all surrounded by those gold and burgundy fall flowers his mom loved. He'd have to ask her what they were called.

Eclectic. That was how he'd describe the setting. Each bar stool, every chair and table, was different. Walls covered with art from local artists along with black and white old-time pictures of the town of Amery. A small bookshelf beneath the front window sported a sign that read, "Take a Book. Leave a Book."

With the music, art, and literature displayed, supporting the arts community was apparently important to the owner. Nate would work that into his design.

He took out a sketchbook and began drawing up some plans. While he loved working on his Mac, sometimes the best ideas came from pencil drawings.

A guitar strummed, and a familiar voice welcomed guests to Roasted to a Tea. Startled, Nate looked over at the stage, his mouth agape.

Tessa?

In some really cute Bohemian outfit.

And a black boot on her injured foot.

Not wanting her to see him and be a distraction, he moved his chair and hunched down, hoping the group in front of him provided decent cover.

"My name's Tessitura, and I'm excited to sing for you tonight."

Excited and nervous, apparently. He could hear her voice shake as she gripped the microphone stand. Even her fingers had turned white.

Tessitura. What a perfect name for a musician.

"Thanks to Ben for inviting me, and thank you all for coming. I'm going to be singing several songs that might be familiar to you, and a few of my own. Hope you enjoy them. And don't forget to enjoy the amazing coffee, tea, and pastry selections."

She began with a soulful "It is Well," and moved into "Amazing Grace." She followed those up with a ballad he'd never heard before, singing about searching for a savior and finding him in false dreams and lies and finally discovering true freedom in the only One who could offer it.

Wow . . .

The emotion in her music and lyrics had the crowd sniffling and made him almost tear up.

She did a few more songs. Some popular pieces she'd rearranged and changed lyrics to point to God instead of a boy- or girlfriend relationship, a few more hymns, and another original. And all too soon she was done.

"I'll be back a week from today. Hope to see you then. And you're all welcome back tomorrow night for a worship service. Have a great evening."

She stepped off the stage to wild applause and was instantly surrounded with fans.

And he just sat there, numb, wanting to pull her away from the crowd, wanting to hear her story.

Not tonight, though. He'd wait until tomorrow evening when he had time to prepare and try to figure out what his heart was telling him.

He stuffed his sketchbook into his messenger bag, along

with his laptop. While Tessa was busy talking with fans, he snuck out the front door. He couldn't wait to talk with her tomorrow. Hopefully, she'd want to talk to him.

With a crowd of people surrounding Tessa, she watched a tall, curly-haired blond guy squeeze between the crowds at Roasted to a Tea and out the front door.

Nate?

Couldn't be. He would have said something to her, wouldn't he? But then, maybe the way she'd left the Brooks home, maybe the way she'd told him to leave her alone, had sealed the casket on their friendship.

Why did he show up now when she'd just learned amazing news: her parents were singing in Iowa? They were only a state away. The Chanson Family Singers still didn't have a website, but the church they were singing at did. Knowing her family was that close had made it difficult singing tonight, but the crowd still loved her.

After all those years of Jared telling her she couldn't sing. Why had she believed all his lies?

And why did memories of him still intrude?

She banished his name and face once again and smiled for the crowd gathered around her. After chatting with everyone who'd stayed, she packed her guitar into its case.

It was time to head to Our Home and pray.

About what to do with her parents.

About what to do with Nate.

She'd love to tell him what his friendship had meant to her, how he'd played an instrumental part in getting her to look for freedom in Christ. She wanted to see his eyes light up as she told him about teaching and about her plans to go to college. He'd be so proud of her. His entire family would be.

She was pretty pleased with herself.

"Tessa, you were amazing!" Keisha bounded up to her and wrapped her in a hug. Then quickly let her go. "Oh, sorry. I just can't help myself."

"It's okay." Tessa was even beginning to look forward to Keisha's hugs. "And thank you."

"The crowd loved you, too. What a debut!"

"It wasn't too bad." The response had been more than what she'd anticipated. After all, she was really doing worship songs. Didn't people listen to the lyrics? Well, even if they didn't, God's voice would speak to them. How cool to be a vessel that God would use! She wanted to tell Nate that as well.

"Not too bad? Not too bad! Girl, you are the queen of understatements." Keisha took the guitar case. "Ready to go?"

Tessa yawned in answer. "Guess it's been a long day. You sure you're up for bringing me tomorrow?"

"For a worship service? You bet! I think all of Our Home will be there."

"That would be nice." Tessa tried to put enthusiasm into her statement.

"Nice . . ." Keisha shook her head and led the way outside. The sky had turned dark since she'd arrived, but streetlamps lit up the avenue. "What's wrong? Is this about finding your parents? Even with that, you were all excited for this, and it went better than any of us anticipated, and now you sound like you just lost your best friend."

With her good foot, Tessa kicked at a piece of loose concrete. "I think maybe I did."

"Say what?" Keisha stood still.

Tessa pointed to a nearby bench, so she could rest. "Remember that guy I told you about, the one whose family took me in?"

"Yeah. The really cute one?"

"I guess." She felt her cheeks heat. Thank goodness it was dark, or Keisha would definitely say something.

"What about him?"

She looked up and down the street, and studied the parking lot across the way, looking for an old red pickup. "I think he was here tonight."

"What? And you didn't talk with him?"

"I didn't see him until he was heading out."

"Well, you're gonna give that boy a call tomorrow and invite him to worship."

"I don't know."

"You don't know what? All I've heard since you moved in was 'Nate this' and 'Nate that.' If you don't call him, I will."

Tessa grasped Keisha's hand. "Please don't." Then she released it and folded her hands together. "I need to pray about it first. That's what you all have taught me, right?"

"Fine, now you listen to us! But know that I'm praying too, and I intend to act on His response."

Tessa hoped they both got the same answer. What she didn't tell Keisha, was that she was praying Nate would come without the invitation. That would tell her what she needed to know: that he still cared for her, and that her careless ending of their friendship hadn't permanently closed the door between them.

Chapter Nineteen

Would people return for an evening of worship at Roasted to a Tea? Tessa stared out the window of the business onto a sidewalk empty of people. Maybe she'd be singing to a vacant room tonight. No, not vacant. She'd be singing to God. That was what her music really was about.

She unpacked her guitar, and with it she unpacked thoughts of her parents. Would they call her—rather, would they call Caroline? This morning, she'd left a message at the church they were singing at, said she'd love to get in touch, and left Caroline's phone number. For four years she'd hoped they'd make the first move, but she'd banished pride once again to reach out to them. Keisha had Tessa's phone tonight, just in case they called.

She played a chord on her guitar and winced. Amazing how quickly it went out of tune.

Not too different from people, she'd learned. Four years of avoiding the Bible and prayer and turning her back on God had made her go seriously out of tune. But now, the Master Tuner was doing His thing, and her life was no longer a discordant mess.

She tightened a few strings, loosened others, and soon her guitar had that full, blended sound she loved. If it weren't for Nate, would she have given a thought to singing for an audience?

Nate . . .

She sighed. Would he be here tonight? She hadn't called him, much to the chagrin of Keisha, but she hadn't received a firm answer to her prayers. Maybe that man she'd seen leave Roasted to a Tea hadn't been Nate. Maybe she'd seen only what she'd wanted to see.

She picked out the intro to "In Christ Alone." Her cover would be similar to the version on the radio, so people could sing along. *If* people came tonight. This was Ben's—the owner of Roasted to a Tea—first worship service, so it might just be the two of them and Keisha.

Tessa owed her big time for all the chauffeuring she'd done over the past weeks. This coming Friday, her boot would come off, and then Tessa would need transportation to get to and from physical therapy three times a week. She hated being dependent on so many people.

Ben sat down beside her and flung a towel over his shoulder. "You're sounding good."

"It's not about me."

"Tessa." Ben shook his head. "Here's where you say, 'Thank you.'"

She relaxed the guitar between her knees and looked to Ben, a pastor and family man in his mid-thirties who wanted to have a different kind of church, one that would draw in anyone off the street. He'd told her she was an answer to prayer.

Never would she have imagined that she would be prayer's answer.

Ben handed her a sheet of paper with scribblings all over it. "Here's the schedule for tonight. Hope you can read it. My new job doesn't come with a secretary." He winked. "And my wife refuses to fill that role."

She managed to decipher most of his scribblings, enough to know that the three songs she'd prepared were just right. Keisha had created a PowerPoint with the words, and they'd borrowed the projector and screen from Our Home for the evening.

"Looks good." She handed back the paper.

"Now all we need are worshippers." He got up, walked to the front door, and unlocked it. Seconds later Keisha strutted in followed by Rachel, Nancy and her husband, and the two guys from Our Home. Several strangers straggled in, and soon the tables and chairs were full.

But no sign of Nate.

Right at seven P.M., Ben got up and welcomed everyone and then introduced Tessa as his worship team. Rather than stand on the stage, she remained in her chair off to the side, and the words to "Blessed Be Your Name" appeared on the screen. She started off singing loudly, just to encourage others to sing along, then she backed off as worshipers took over the song, making it all about glorifying Him instead of about her.

The door to Roasted to a Tea squeaked and Tessa's gaze flew to it even as she continued to play.

Caroline? Oh, my goodness! Her fingers pressed on wrong strings, making funky chords. *Get it together, Tessa.* She'd speak with her friend later. Her focus back on the music and worship, she finished the song without another mistake. Then she motioned for Caroline to come sit by her. She gave her friend a hug—which surprised Caroline. Her counselor had told her that her fear of touch was due to Jared's control of her. Not showing physical affection to others was her way of taking control over one aspect of her life.

Ben read from the Bible before Tessa led another song, then he began his sermon surrounding Philippians 2:1-11 talking about Jesus' humility. Even as the Savior, He was humble.

Hard to believe she'd once considered Jared to be her savior. That man was the epitome of arrogance. Obviously, he was broken too, and just as much in need of a savior as she had been. Maybe it was time she prayed for him too and learned to forgive him.

But that did not mean she'd return to him. If only she could find a way into his house and retrieve her locket . . .

Ben closed the sermon with a prayer, and Tessa led one more song before the service officially ended, and she could properly welcome her old friend.

Caroline gave her another hug, and no painful tingles crawled over her skin.

"Do you have any idea how beautiful that was? Do you know that God is rejoicing that you're finally using your gifts?"

"Didn't we just hear a sermon on humility?" Tessa set her guitar on its stand.

"Acknowledging your gifts and using them isn't boastful, it's being obedient and thankful."

"You're right." Tessa heaved in a breath and blew it out. "You're absolutely right. That's what Ben's been trying to teach me." She knocked her head with her fist. "Sometime, it will sink in." She lowered her voice to a whisper. "Anything new from Jared?"

Caroline shook her head. "All's quiet over there. Hasn't graced our doorstep for weeks. Hopefully, he's moved on."

Yes, hopefully. "That's good news."

"Well I'd love to stay and chat longer, but I'm beat. I'll come up sometime with the kiddos and take you out to lunch."

"I'd love that."

They exchanged another hug before Caroline said goodbye. Tessa put her guitar in its case and snapped it shut.

"Nice guitar."

Tessa startled and wheeled toward the familiar voice.

"Nate." When had he snuck in?

He smiled that adorably crooked smile. "I know you said stay away, but I heard you last night and I . . . " He combed his fingers through his curls. "I just had to tell you how proud I am of you. How happy I am for you. You were amazing." He turned as if to leave.

"Don't go, Nate."

He stopped, then turned only his head. "Are you sure?"

"Please." She patted the chair beside her. "I have so much to tell you, and there's so much I need to catch up on."

"Well, if that's the case." He grinned and sat beside her.

And then they were talking about her time at Our Home and her renewal of faith and her healing ankle and him finishing The Draken and finding new jobs and how his cat Falcon missed her and how watching Marvel movies wasn't nearly as fun without her.

"You two about done?"

Tessa blinked as her gaze flicked to the bar area where Ben sat with a newspaper in hand.

"I've read everything twice now." He tossed the paper into a metal can marked 'recycle.'

She glanced at the clock and around the now-empty room, and then back at Nate. They'd been talking for over an hour.

"Sorry about that." Nate got up and offered his hand to Tessa. She gladly accepted his help. "We were doing a lot of catching up."

"I see that." Ben smirked. "And I'd love to support your reunion, but my wife is getting anxious for me to come home."

"No problem." Tessa reached for her guitar, but Nate took it and they headed for the front door.

"Looks like your ride home left." He opened the door for her.

"Oh." Tessa looked back into the store then across the street at the parking lot, which was empty but for a red pickup and Keisha's beater. "Oh, no. She's gonna be livid that I've kept her waiting." She hobbled quick as she could toward the car.

"Slow down there." Nate hurried beside her. "I don't want you hurting yourself again."

"Listen to the man." Keisha poked her head outside her car window. "Take your time, Tess. I'm in no hurry."

"You sure?"

"Tessitura . . . " Keisha gave her a look that equaled Nancy's when someone talked back or said or did something she didn't like.

"Okay, okay."

She slowed and walked side by side with Nate to his pickup,

silence taking over. Now what? Did they go their own ways? Would he want to see her again? If he did, she was ready. He may have rescued her that day, but he hadn't ever claimed to be her savior. Hadn't ever tried to take over her life. She realized that now, but she'd needed the distant perspective in order to see clearly.

At the pickup, he stuck hands in his pockets. "I've had fun tonight. I know it's late, but I've got next Friday night open, do you suppose—"

The ringer went off on her phone, and she held up her hand while she looked at it, then answered. "Caroline?"

"Hey hon, while I was away from home, hubby took a call."

Tessa froze. "My parents."

"Yep. And guess what. They're canceling their tour for the week and coming to Minneapolis. They want to see you, Tessa."

Her hand flew to her mouth, and she looked up at the multitude of stars in the sky. What should she do? "I need to think. Can I call you right back?"

"It's been four years. Take all the time you need."

Nate leaned against his pickup. "You okay?"

She pocketed her phone and paced. "I don't know. I don't know what to do." Why did they want to see her now after four years of ignoring her?

"Can I ask a question?" Nate crossed a leg over the other.

She shrugged. "You can ask." But that didn't mean she was going to answer.

"What's the deal with your parents? I know Jared was a scumbag, but you've never said anything about them. What did they do to you?"

She stood still and looked up at Nathan, fighting anger and tears. "I grew up on the road, on a bus, and all I ever wanted was a home like every other child out there. I wanted to go to school and make friends and go to prom and football games, but never had the opportunity. Until Jared came along." She wiped a hand across her eyes. "He offered me a home. Freedom." She spat out the word. "And then they disowned me. Once I ran away with Jared, I never heard from them again. They never responded to any letters. Four years, and now they want to see me?"

Nate scratched the side of his head. "Is that how they were growing up? Unforgiving?"

She sighed and stared at the asphalt. "No, and that's why it hurt so badly. They always preached forgiveness, but then didn't give it to me."

"Are you sure?"

"Of course, I'm sure." She glared at Nate. "I just told you, I never, not once, heard from them."

"Yeah, but if this Jared was as controlling as you say he was, what was stopping him from intercepting correspondence?"

Tessa froze and squeezed her eyes shut. Why had she never considered that possibility? "Do you really think that could be true?"

He shrugged. "I don't know them, but you did."

And she'd been so angry with them for stifling her freedom and pleased with herself for being independent. Then Jared had slowly manipulated her thoughts. "I need to give them a chance." She straightened and then opened her arms to Nate.

He stood there, unmoving, as if in shock, then he folded his arms around her and whispered in her ear. "I'm proud of you, Tessa."

Too soon, he released her. "Let me know how it all turns out."

"I promise." She turned around and hustled toward Keisha's car, as fast as the boot allowed her. All she could think of was she was going to see her parents again, and that scared her to death.

It also thrilled her.

Once they heard her story, she'd pray they'd forgive her.

But before she met them, she had one important thing to do.

Find that necklace she'd left at Jared's.

Chapter Twenty

*A*re you sure this is what you want to do?"

Tessa nodded at Caroline while fidgeting with the key in her pocket. If Jared had changed the locks, or installed an alarm, her plan would be foiled, but she had to take the chance. "I have to. That necklace is a family heirloom. They entrusted it to my keeping. And I . . . I lost it."

"Or Jerkwad took it."

Which is what she feared the most.

Well, that, or his discovering her at his house. She shivered at the thought, but she wasn't going to let him stop her. Not again. She'd stand up to him and not let him mess with her mind.

She checked the clock on Caroline's kitchen wall. Ten A.M. She'd better go now or forget it. "He's at work right now." If he hadn't changed his schedule—which he hadn't in the four-plus years she'd known him.

"Okay. Don't forget I'll ring once if I see him. And use the flashlight on your phone instead of turning on lights."

"I'm not a child."

Caroline sighed. "I know." She pushed her toward the back door. "Go. I'll be watching."

"Praying too?"

"I haven't stopped. Stay safe, Tessa."

Tessa prayed she would.

Nate hurried to his monthly meeting with his supervisor. Hopefully, all the work he'd been doing on the side hadn't compromised his work here. He still needed the job. Just as he reached the door to the meeting room, his phone vibrated. He pulled it from his pocket to turn it off but seeing Caroline's name stopped him. She wouldn't contact him if it wasn't important.

With a minute to spare before his meeting, he answered her call. "This is Nate."

"Oh, thank goodness you answered. It's Tessa. She's going to Jared's. Wants to find a locket she left behind, and I don't like it."

He didn't either. Warning bells went off in his brain. After talking to the owner of I-Spy Home Security the other day, Nate realized Jared would know the second Tessa stepped onto his property. "Is anyone with her?"

"She's alone, and I've got my kids."

"I'll be right out. What's the address?"

Caroline relayed it, and they hung up.

Then he called 911 and told them about a domestic abuse situation happening now. He prayed he was lying to them—he'd gladly take the punishment for making a false report—but his gut told him he was telling them the truth.

He couldn't rescue her from this. Actually, he wasn't responsible for saving anyone. That was God's job. Just as Bridget's death hadn't been his fault. She'd made her own, deadly choice in spite of the warnings she'd received from him and others.

Outside the meeting room, Nate got on his knees and prayed Tessa hadn't made the same deadly choice. Saving her wasn't up to him—never had been. That was completely in God's hands.

Tessa could already feel herself perspire as she limped to the gate between Caroline's yard and Jared's. If only she didn't have this clunker of a boot on, she'd be stealthier, but she didn't have a choice.

Holding her breath, she tried the latch on the gate. It moved. It lifted! She released her breath and pulled the gate open just enough to peek through. Nothing moved in the yard. No lights were on in the house.

Time to go.

She squeezed through the opening and closed the gate behind her, then she hobbled across the perfectly manicured yard to the back door of Jared's house. From her pocket, she removed a key she'd given Caroline months ago, just in case.

Her hand shook as she tried inserting the key into the lock. The key fell from her hands and rattled on the concrete step. "Get it together, Tessa," she mumbled under her breath as she bent to pick up the key.

Again, she aimed for the lock, and a dog barked from next door. She startled, but this time didn't drop the key. "Steady, Tessa, you can do this." She focused on the deadbolt, shoved the key in, then held her breath as she attempted to turn it to the left.

It resisted.

She ground her teeth and tried harder.

It freed.

And she released her breath as she pried it the rest of the way. Now to see if he'd installed an alarm, which she wouldn't put past him.

Every muscle in her body tensed as she gripped the doorknob.

And turned it, waiting for the shrill sound of an alarm.

That never came.

Once again, she breathed easier. God had to be on her side.

She stepped into the home she'd once thought was a castle. Four bedrooms, three baths, a chef's kitchen, and so much more. It had turned out to be no more than a fancy prison she'd allowed herself to be caged in.

Never again.

She walked through the mudroom into the kitchen. Then through the living room and upstairs to the master bedroom complete with a fireplace dressed with stacked stone. Once upon a time, she'd thought it romantic.

Now it gave her the shivers.

She banished the images and focused on her goal: find the necklace. The last place she'd seen it, only days before she'd fled, was the bottom of her jewelry box.

That was still as empty as the day she'd left. Maybe she'd

accidentally put it in a different spot. She opened the top drawer and dug through expensive jewelry he'd given her, usually as an apology, but nothing was there. The second and third drawers didn't have it either. She rummaged through her dresser drawers and Jared's. Through the side table drawers, through the closet, through each drawer in the master bedroom.

Nothing. Yet. She'd find it if she had to search through every nook in this house. This was one time Tessa was grateful she hadn't had a lot of personal items. This house had no clutter, and therefore less to search through.

She hunted through the remaining upstairs bedrooms and bathrooms and came up empty.

On the main floor, she searched every cabinet and drawer in the kitchen and powder room. In the living room, she even checked beneath the lampshades and behind and under the furniture. That left his office, which he'd always kept locked.

But with her not around, maybe that had changed. She hurried from the living room to the office at the front of the house. She could see into the room through the French doors, taunting her. She tried the doorknob.

It turned! Now to see what he'd kept so private in this sparsely decorated room. No computer—he always took his laptop with him. No bookshelves. No file cabinets. Just a desk with a single tiny drawer in the front. She tugged on the drawer handle.

And it eased open. Yes!

But it only opened a short way. She reached in and felt nothing, but that wasn't going to deter her. She took out her phone, turned on the flashlight, and shined it into the drawer.

There! A chain and what looked like a locket, spread against the back of the drawer. Now to get it out. She hurried to the kitchen and found a fork then returned to the office.

She squeezed the fork into the space and drug out the chain.

And she groaned.

Just a cheap, rusting chain with nothing attached. It had probably been there for years. She shone the flashlight in the drawer again. What she'd thought was a locket was just a label on the back of the drawer. She returned the chain to its hiding place.

All that was left to search now was the unfinished basement that had always given her the creeps. This house had been renovated before Jared purchased it. All but the basement. That still had cobwebbed walls and the remnants of an old furnace with chubby octopus arms.

All too often, Jared had threatened to throw her in the basement but had never followed through.

She could do this, but not alone. She looked upward and pleaded with one word, "Help" then she opened the heavy wood door and stared down into blackness.

Her heart rate doubled as she turned on her phone flashlight again. Rickety wood stairs led down. Was the locket worth this?

Yes, yes it was. But she had better hurry. Staying longer was begging to be caught. Flashlight aimed straight ahead, she took the steps faster than she should have.

Her boot caught on the bottom step, and she fell face first to the concrete floor, and the phone flew away. It hit the floor and cracked open.

Everything went dark.

And something crawled across her arm.

No, no, no! The necklace wasn't worth this. Not at all. Her parents would forgive her, and if they didn't, that wasn't her problem.

She got to her knees, then sat up and checked her boot. It was still tight. Now to make it up these stairs without incident. At least she had the light from the main floor guiding her way.

She climbed the steps. One. Two . . . Six. Seven.

The door above creaked all the way open.

And there stood Jared.

"Looking for this?" He dangled a chain with a heart-shaped locket from his fingers.

Her breath hitched then came out in rushing waves.

"Let me through, Jared. You can keep the locket."

"You think I want this?" He hurled it past her, and it tinked on the floor below. "Go ahead, get it."

"I don't—"

"I said, get it." He raised his other hand and pointed a gun at her. "Like my new purchase? I've been taking target practice. The instructor says I'm a natural." She heard a click, and his voice turned cold. "Get. The. Chain."

Her mouth went dry. "Then you'll let me go?"

"We'll see."

Perspiration dripped down her spine as she backed down the stairs to the basement floor. Without lights on, she could see nothing, so she got on her hands and knees and felt around the cold, pitted, slimy, dusty concrete floor.

"Why'd you do it, Tessa?" That familiar, tear-filled voice came from above. "Why'd you leave me? I gave you everything. Every. Thing!" His voice echoed through the basement.

Quivering, she looked up at Jared, a dark shadow surrounded by a halo of light, as her fingers searched the grimy floor. Something skittered across her hand, and she yelped.

"You never did like creepy-crawlies."

She swallowed hard as her fingers kept searching. "Neither did you."

"No. I didn't." He took one step toward her. "Why'd you do it, Tessa? You know I can't live without you." He sniffled. "I love you."

How often had she heard those lines, followed by the threat of what he'd do to himself if she ever left?

Her fingers landed on something hard. Heart-shaped? She pinched it between her fingers and lifted.

Her locket! "I've got it." She tucked it into her jeans pocket.

"I always knew you'd come back for it."

Fear pulsed down her spine. "Now you'll let me go?" Her voice shook.

He stepped back from beneath the door frame and grasped the door.

"No!" She crawled toward the stairs. "Please don't lock me down here. Please."

"You think I'm a monster."

"No. No you're not." She slowly crawled up the steps, pleading for God's help. "I think you're someone who wants to be loved."

"You never loved me." He wiped his hand across his face—the hand with the gun.

"Yes, I did." Or she'd loved the idea of him. She managed to stand on shaky legs and climbed a few more steps.

He backed away. To close the door or to let her through?

"But you left anyway." His voice trembled.

"I had to Jared, you were . . . I needed my freedom."

"You can have it. I promise."

"You do?" If it took lying to him to get out of this, she'd fib all day. "I can sing again?"

He sniffled. "Yes."

"What I want to sing?"

His silence stopped her. Then with the gun in his hand, he waved her up the remaining steps. He shut the door behind her and aimed the weapon at her. "Go."

She gulped as he motioned for her to go through the living room, then up the stairs to his bedroom. Then onto the bed. He wouldn't . . .

"Don't do this, Jared, please." She tucked her good leg tight against her body and wrapped her arms around it as if that would keep him away. "I'll come back to you."

He stepped to the end of the bed.

Bile climbing her throat, she backed against the headboard. "You don't want to do this, Jared. You never wanted to hurt me."

"No, I didn't. But you left anyway."

"I'll come back."

He laughed and gripped the gun with both hands, steadying his aim on her. "I'm not stupid, Tessa. I know you won't stay." His finger tightened on the trigger.

Her entire body shook. "Don't, Jared." She sat up and inched toward him. If she was going to die now, at least she'd be with Jesus. She had to let him know. "I left because you caged me. You took away my freedom, my independence. You took away who I am. I've finally rediscovered who I am: a child of God, and if you shoot me, I'll be with Jesus. That can happen for you, too. Jesus loves you, Jared."

The gun shook in his hands, and he laughed.

She moved closer to him. "You're not a monster. You never hurt me before. Don't do it now. Get help. Talk to a counselor. You do this, I'll be with Jesus, but you'll spend the rest of your life in prison, and I know you don't want that."

Chin quivering, he lowered the gun to his side. "You're right." He wiped a hand across his nose then raised up the gun and jutted it against his temple. "If I can't have you, I don't want to live."

"Jared, no—"

Chapter Twenty-One

D on't do it, Jared, please!" Tessa crawled toward him.

"Put the gun down," a voice came from behind Jared. A police officer? Where had he come from?

Jared's gaze slipped from Tessa, and he slowly turned toward the door, the gun not moving from his head.

The officer stood beneath the doorframe, the gun in his hand down to his side. The officer looked incredibly calm, as if he was stopping in to chat.

While she was shaking hard enough to jiggle the bed.

"Let Tessa go, Jared. You don't want to hurt her."

Jared pressed the gun tighter to his head. "I wasn't going to hurt her." He began sobbing. "I never laid a hand on her."

"That's good. Just let your girlfriend leave, then you and I can have a talk."

Jared's gaze flitted to Tessa then back to the officer. "I wasn't going to hurt her."

"I know. Back away from the bed." The officer remained relaxed. How did he do that?

Jared gulped and finally did as he was told.

"Good job."

The officer took one step into the room, leaving just enough space for her to escape through. He made a small motion with his free hand, telling her to hurry around him.

She got off the bed and limped past the officer. And gasped. Another policeman stood inside the hallway's shadows, his gun aimed at Jared's head. With steely eyes, he motioned for her to get out of his way. Didn't have to tell her twice. She slipped around him and looked back. How had she not seen him? Too focused on Jared maybe? And the first officer?

Get going, Tessa!

Heart still threatening to beat out of her chest, she hobbled down the stairs, lifting prayers for Jared the entire time.

Why had she been so stingy with her prayers for him?

Because she was selfish, just like when she'd run away from home.

She hurried out the back door, and it slammed behind her.

A gun shot rang out.

She screamed and grabbed the back of her head and cowered on the steps.

Arms came around her, lifting her. "Let's get you to Caroline's." Nate?

She threw her arms around his neck as he ran across the yard and through the gate. Caroline locked it behind him. He carried her to the deck and tried putting her down in a patio chair, but she gripped him tighter and buried her face into his neck as tears streamed from her eyes.

Jared . . . Was he dead? It was her fault. If she had left well enough alone, not worried about the locket, he'd still be okay.

Nate sat, keeping her on his lap. "You're safe, Tessa. You're okay. He's not going to hurt you ever again."

Tears came as relief calmed her pulse and loosened her muscles.

But her heart still grieved for Jared.

Chapter Twenty-Two

Tessa fingered the locket—a heart-shaped music box locket that played "Jesus Saves"—as she walked boot-free across the park, alongside Nate. After four years, she was finally going to be reunited with her parents.

Had they forgiven her for running away? Could she forgive them for abandoning her? If they had indeed abandoned her?

She spotted them at a picnic table not far from the children's play area, right where they said they'd be.

"I'll wait here." Nate pointed to benches surrounding a sand volleyball court where a game was going on.

"Thank you." Tessa breathed in deeply and tried to loosen her tightening muscles as she neared her family. She got within a table's length and stopped. Obvious tears rolled down her mother's face, and her father's eyes were glassy. That meant they'd missed her, right?

"Tessitura?" Her mother covered her mouth with her hand then rushed toward her and enveloped her with a hug.

Tessa stiffened, and then relaxed as her father joined in the hug.

"Oh, how we've missed you." Her mother stepped back,

shaking her head, keeping her hands on Tessa's shoulders. "You're not our little girl anymore." She swiped a curl from Tessa's forehead. "Are you okay? Caroline told us about Jared having a gun."

Her dad's jaw tightened. "He's lucky I wasn't there to—"

"Edward."

Well some things never changed. Her mom was still able to silence her dad with a single word.

"I'm fine." She motioned toward the table, and her parents sat on both sides of her. This way she didn't have to look at their faces and see the emotion there. "I'm scheduled to go to a counselor to deal with it and to work out these past years."

"Did he hurt you?" Her dad's voice was gruff as he lifted her chin, drawing her gaze to his eyes. The protector she remembered. But back then she hadn't appreciated his protection, especially whenever some guy talked to her. Now to answer her father's question honestly.

"He didn't hurt me. Physically." She stared off at the playground on the other side of the volleyball court. If she hadn't miscarried Cadence, her little girl could be swinging over there.

"And how is Jared doing?" Mother's concern didn't surprise Tessa. Her mom had always cared for everyone.

"His foot's healing, I guess." The cop had convinced Jared to lower his gun, and then he accidentally shot his foot. Served him right. "He's been transferred to a behavioral institution. What happens from there, I don't know. I know I should care, but I don't. Maybe that's something I have to work out with the counselor."

She picked at imaginary lint on her skirt. "I need to know

something." That would help her heal whether she liked the answer or not. "Did you try writing me? Contacting me?"

"You never got our letters?"

Guess that answered her question. She leaned over and plucked blades of grass. "He must have intercepted them. Did you get mine?"

"No, we didn't, and we took that to mean you didn't want us to bother you." Tessa had never heard such sadness—regret—in her mother's voice. "We should have tried harder."

Tessa laughed sarcastically. "Well, when I tell you to leave me alone . . . "

"But we did write letters, hoping." Her dad took her hand. "We continuously prayed for this moment."

"Then you can forgive me?"

"Oh, honey." Her mother wrapped her in a hug. "We forgave you the second you left." She released the hug and leaned back. "Can you forgive us for not seeing that you needed a life beyond our travels?"

"You were just trying to protect me."

"And clipped your wings in the process." Her mother took her other hand. "Can you forgive us?"

"Already done."

Tessa looked up at the trees in their full autumn splendor. A masterpiece painted by God.

"Would you consider joining us again?" Her mother squeezed her hand. "Caroline said you've written music. We'd love to incorporate that into our ministry."

Tessa sighed, hating to disappoint her parents. "I think God has a different ministry in mind. I had been thinking of spending time at Auntie Shay's cabin." Part of her still longed to go there, but that was the runaway in her. One thing she'd learned over the past several weeks was that home wasn't a physical place, but a matter of heart. A matter of faith. As long as she placed her faith and trust in Jesus, her heart always had a home.

Her gaze flicked to Nate. Maybe her heart had room for someone else too.

"Oh, you don't know." Her mom shook her head. "My crazy sister sold the cabin for far too much money and is traveling the world. That 'cabin' is now a mini-mansion."

"Oh." Tessa shook her head then began laughing with joy over God's provision. If she'd made it up to the cabin, she'd still be homeless. "Boy, I'm glad Nate's family took me in."

"That's the young man who came with you?" It figured, that was what her dad was concerned about.

"Yes, that's Nate. Nathan Brooks."

"Is he the one who rescued you?" Also, no surprise, that question came from her mom.

"Yes, he is." In more ways than one. From the minute he picked her up from the roadside, to being the one to call the police when she went to Jared's house, he'd been rescuing her.

"Sounds like someone I want to meet." Her father stood up and motioned for Nate to join them.

Tessa's gut churned as he jogged toward them. Her relationship with him was still undetermined. She liked him, all right. Okay, really liked him, but they hadn't even been on a date. If he asked her out, though, no doubt she'd say 'yes.'

Nate reached their table and right away showed his adorable grin while offering his hand. "Nate Brooks."

"Edward Chanson, and this is my wife, Crescendo."

Her mom extended her hand. "Please call me Cress."

"Nice to meet you both."

Her dad motioned for Nate to sit on the other side of the table. Real nice. Him facing the three of them like some inquisition? That was why boys had never made it past 'Hello' with her.

She mouthed 'sorry' to him, but he just grinned bigger, and made hummingbirds flit around her stomach. That had never happened with Jared.

Her dad folded his hands on the wood-slatted table. "Tessitura tells us you've had a large impact on her life."

"Well." He shrugged and scratched the side of his head. "Just doing what God calls me to do."

"Good answer."

Tessa rolled her eyes. Her dad hadn't changed. She never wanted him to.

"So now tell me." Dad turned on his gruff voice and leaned closer to Nate. Nate backed away. "What are your intentions toward my daughter?"

Nate's eyes grew large as a guitar pick, and he squirmed. "I . . . uh . . . " He looked wide-eyed at Tessa, but then settled, and a determined, confident look took over his face. "Mr. and Mrs. Chanson, I like your daughter very much." He looked directly at Tessa and winked. "Very, very much actually, and I'd like to have your permission to date her."

Say what?

He grinned, and she felt her face heat with a blush.

"Date her, huh?" Her dad leaned further across the table. This time Nate leaned toward her father. "And then?"

"Sir, I can't answer that now. I barely know her, and she's

been through so much these past years, but I want to know her better. What I do know is that I care for Tessa very much. She's smart and independent and funny and sings like an angel and I enjoy being around her. But I'll also assure you that I will never take advantage of her or control her or come between the three of you. I'll always put her needs first and treat her like the princess she is."

Her father nodded, and a smile twitched on his face. "Thank you, Nate, and yes, you have permission to date my daughter, if Tessa agrees."

She reached across the table.

Nate stared at her open hand for a milli-second then grasped it.

His grip felt secure, loving. "Nathan Brooks, I'd love to date you, too, as long as you don't hide your flaws from me."

He laughed. "No problem there, Tessa. Believe me, I'm no Captain America."

"No, you're not." Her heart sang at the possibility of another chance at love. Real, unconditional love. "You're better."

"Behold, God is my salvation;
I will trust, and will not be afraid;
for the Lord God is my strength and my song,
and he has become my salvation."

Isaiah 12:2

Dear Reader,

Thank you for reading Tessa and Nate's story. It wasn't easy writing about an abusive relationship, but I know there are far too many who can relate to Tessa, and each is an important story to tell. Always remember, through Jesus, there is healing!

If you enjoyed **Place Called Home**, please consider sharing a book review, telling other readers why you liked this story. The review doesn't have to be long or eloquent, just honest.

You'll find further inspiration and encouragement at www.PottersHouseBooks.com and by reading other books in this uplifting series. Find all the books on Amazon and on The Potter's House Books website.

To be notified of all my new releases, join my email list at BrendaAndersonBooks.com/Subscribe. As a Thank You for subscribing, you will receive a FREE copy of **Coming Home**, a Coming Home Series short story.

Thank you for joining me on this writing journey!

In Him,

Brenda

Acknowledgements

Thank you to the six other Potter's House Books authors who welcomed me into the fold. It's an honor writing alongside all of you!

Thank you, Book Booster Team, for tirelessly spreading the word about my books!

Thank you, Danielle Erhard, for walking me through what happens when you fracture an ankle. Ouch!

Thank you, Joseph Courtemanche, for your help in understanding police procedures. Any mistakes are my own!

Thank you, Stacy Monson, Stephanie Prichard, Ginny Yttrup, and Sarah Anderson, for your immensely helpful critiques! My story and characters are far stronger due to your insight.

Thank you, Gayle Balster, for always daring to read my first drafts. Your thoughts and support are tremendous encouragement!

Thanks to my three children, Sarah, Bryan, and Brandon, for helping me really know the true meaning of home.

Thanks to my husband, Marvin, for your unending, enthusiastic support! I couldn't do this without you!

And thank you, Jesus, our one true Savior and mighty healer, for blessing me with the gift of story. It's my prayer that readers will see You among the pages.

Other Potter's House Books

By Brenda S. Anderson

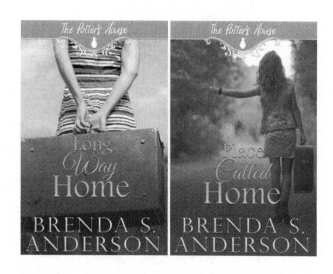

Long Way Home

Place Called Home

Home Another Way

(coming February 2019)

Find all the Potter's House Books at:

http://pottershousebooks.com/our-books/

Book 1: **The Homecoming** by Juliette Duncan

Book 2: **When it Rains** by T.K. Chapin

Book 3: **Heart Unbroken** by Alexa Verde

Book 4: **Long Way Home** by Brenda S. Anderson

Book 5: **Promises Renewed** by Mary Manners

Book 6: **A Vow Redeemed** by Kristen M. Fraser

Book 7: **Restoring Faith** by Marion Ueckermann

Book 8: **Unchained** by Juliette Duncan

Book 9: **Gracefully Broken** by T.K. Chapin

Book 10: **Heart Healed** by Alexa Verde

Book 11: **Place Called Home** by Brenda S. Anderson

Book 12: **Tragedy & Trust** by Mary Manners

Book 13: **Heart Transformed** by Kristen M. Fraser

Book 14: **Recovering Hope** by Marion Ueckermann

Books 15 – 21 To Be Announced . . .

Find all of Brenda S. Anderson's books at:
www.BrendaAndersonBooks.com/books

Coming Home Series

Praise for the Coming Home Series

"Anderson tackles family dynamics, tough issues, and gritty realism in her Coming Home series. From special needs babies to abortion and homelessness, you'll root for her authentic characters as they face real life struggles."

— Award-winning author, **Shannon Taylor Vannatter**

" . . . heartfelt, heart-wrenching fiction at its best, exploring relationships and family, love, faith and forgiveness in fresh, life-changing ways. I see myself in these endearing, enduring characters, their weaknesses and struggles and hard-won triumphs."

— **Laura Frantz**, author of *A Moonbow Night*

"Anderson thrusts her readers into the gritty underbelly of family life and she doesn't mince words or shy away from the difficulties that complicate relationships. The reoccurring themes of grace and restitution are delivered with heart-wrenching honesty. These compelling stories celebrate the joys and sorrows of ordinary living with an extraordinary God."

— **Kav Rees**, BestReads-kav.blogspot.com

Where the Heart Is Series

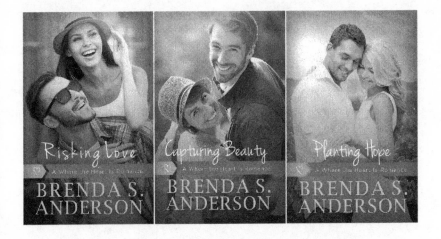

Praise for the Where the Heart Is Series

"*Risking Love* is a touching story of love and loss - and risking your heart! I can't wait to read the next in the series!"

—**Regina Rudd Merrick**, author of *Carolina Dream*

"Brenda does a great job bringing us into the story, capturing our attention and keeping it till the end. I read the first book in this series and look forward to the next. I highly recommend *Capturing Beauty* – it's an inspiring story of second chances and new perspectives!"

—**Angela D. Meyer**, author of *Where Hope Starts*

"*Planting Hope* is a lovely wrap-up to the Where the Heart Is series. The strength, or lack thereof, of a family unit has a profound impact on all of its members. Brenda Anderson expertly illustrates that in this story, and all of her books, as she deals honestly with the idiosyncrasies of families – the good, bad, and ugly. *Planting Hope* is about the hope God plants deep in our hearts, and the lengths we'll go to for those we love."

—Award-winning author, **Stacy Monson**,
author of *Open Circle*

If you enjoyed stories by **Brenda S. Anderson**, you may also enjoy books by **Stacy Monson**

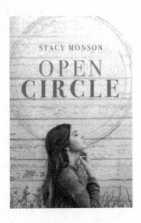

and the

Chain of Lakes Series

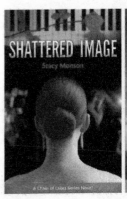

 **Brenda S. Anderson** writes gritty and authentic, life-affirming fiction. She is a member of the American Christian Fiction Writers, and is Past-President of the ACFW Minnesota chapter, MN-NICE, the 2016 ACFW Chapter of the Year. When not reading or writing, she enjoys music, theater, roller coasters, and baseball (Go Twins!), and she loves watching movies with her family. She resides in the Minneapolis, Minnesota area with her husband of 31 years, their three children, and one sassy cat.

Connect with Brenda

Email: Brenda@BrendaAndersonBooks.com
Website: www.BrendaAndersonBooks.com
Newsletter: http://brendaandersonbooks.com/subscribe/
Facebook: facebook.com/BrendaSAndersonAuthor/
Twitter: twitter.com/BrendaSAnders_n
Pinterest: pinterest.com/brendabanderson/
Goodreads: goodreads.com/BrendaSAnderson
BookBub: bookbub.com/authors/brenda-s-anderson